Gloria's Inn

By Robin Alexander

GLORIA'S INN

ISBN 1-933113-01-4

THIS TRADE PAPERBACK ORIGINAL IS PUBLISHED BY INTAGLIO PUBLICATIONS, GAINESVILLE, FL USA

FIRST PRINTING: OCTOBER 2004

CREDITS

EXECUTIVE EDITOR: STACIA SEAMAN

COVER DESIGN: SHERI

Dedication

My first book is dedicated to my family—you all have proven to be more supportive than I ever dreamed. Thank you so much for putting up with me through all of this, especially Phil and Taylor, whom I love with all of my heart.

Amy, this would have never happened had you not nudged—well, shoved me in the right direction. Thank you so much for your support and encouragement. I love you very much.

Acknowledgments

To J.P. Mercer, who took me under her wing and taught me so much. Her initiative made my dream come true. I will be forever grateful to this cherished friend.

To Donna Lorson, my very dear friend, whose support and encouragement keeps me writing.

To Sheri, whose beautiful artwork adorns my cover. I'm so glad I met you, my twin. You will always have a place in my heart.

To Jules, who kept me laughing through this whole process.

To Kathy Smith and Denise Winthrop of Intaglio Publications and StarCrossed Productions for taking a chance on me.

Last, but certainly not least, to Vagabond Manuscript Consultants, who took me by the hand and made all of this go smoothly. Your assistance has been invaluable, and I couldn't have done it without your skillful guidance.

PROLOGUE

I am Hayden Tate, self-proclaimed loner and proud of it. They tell me, though I can't see it, that God and my parents' genes saw fit to bless me with the Tate good looks. I've had my fair share of relationships, not all of which ended with a kiss on the cheek and a "let's do lunch."

Belly up to the bar, I have a story to tell you. I'll bet you're wondering how a girl like me came to own a Bahamian island inn that caters to an alternative lifestyle. Well, it's funny, really. My favorite aunt died, and you guessed it, she left half of Gloria's Inn, located on a tropical paradise called Cat Island, to her favorite niece, who just happens to be me, Hayden Tate. Sounds like a slice of heaven, right? Well, I thought so too— and in some ways I suppose it is.

You see, I'm not really a people person, and the inn business requires you to be up close and personal with your guests. To be honest, most of the time I really have to reach deep down inside and try to be nice. Sometimes I just don't measure up. Perhaps I work too hard at it. But that's where my lovely business partner Adrienne comes into play. More often than not, she has to yank my foot out of my mouth after I have firmly wedged it in.

Ah! Adrienne. Let me tell you about her. Beautiful inside and out, which is the best way I know how to describe her. I do have to admit, though, there was something about her that spooked me and had me ready to run back to New Orleans across bridges that I had just burned. I had concluded that Adrienne was, to put it quite simply, weird.

I found myself involved in intrigue, murder, and the mystery of Cat Island. If you want to hear the rest of the tale, stick around. I promise you will learn the whole story of Gloria's Inn, and you'll meet some mighty interesting characters along the way. Some will make you laugh out loud; others may make you want to run and hide. But enough for now. Can I book a reservation for you at Gloria's Inn?

CHAPTER ONE

O kay, Adrienne, let me see the list."
She handed me the register as I stretched out on the chaise lounge. She shot me a nervous glance as I sipped my coffee and perused the guest list.

"What can you tell me about William Thomason and Christopher Tanner?" When her answer did not come readily, I peered over the book. She was sitting there with a far-off look in her eyes. Something about her behavior made me nervous.

"I really, really hate it when you do that, you know," I said, trying to get her to share what was going on in that head of hers.

She grinned ear to ear at my admission. "Patience is a virtue, dear one."

"I think we both know that I come up short in the patience department. Please humor me and tell me about Thomason." I leaned back in the chair and lit my cigarette.

"Thomason is a jackass."

I waited for her to elaborate. Nothing. I sighed and glanced at the register again. "Richard and Jerri Burke—what about these two?"

"They're a married straight couple looking to incorporate another into their bed."

She pretended to clean the bar that she had already nearly polished the finish off of that very morning. Despite my measures to remain calm, I was on my way to blowing a gasket. Something was up, and she was not sharing it with me.

"The Burkes are cheats and liars. Nothing but trouble. I wish they had chosen somewhere else to play. I don't care for their kind."

While I had her on a roll, I threw the next two names at her. "What about Madyson Taylor and Emily Potter?"

"They're lovers," she said without further comment.

"Okay, fine with me." I scanned down to the next names. "How about Abigail Grigsby and Sandy Winters?"

She grimaced. "Their relationship is on the rocks. They're hoping this trip will rekindle what they once had."

I tried to soften my tone because what I saw in her eyes scared me—I felt helpless to do anything about it. "Annie Pearson and Liz West. Do you have anything on them?"

She sighed. "They've only been together six months, and this is their first vacation together."

"Okay, we're down to the last one. Tell me about Brandon Fallon." She said nothing, simply stared straight ahead.

"Are you okay?" I asked.

"Nothing. I have nothing at all." She went back to polishing the bar.

"What do you mean, nothing? You've never come up with just nothing. Are you sick? Is there something wrong with you?"

She sighed, obviously exasperated. "I don't know what it is, really. I can't get anything on him. This has never happened to me before, and it gives me the worst feeling inside. There's something amiss here, something foreboding about this man. It unnerves me. That much I do know. But I just can't put my finger on it."

"We can refuse his business, you know. We don't have to let him stay here." She was giving me the creeps. I didn't want this guy staying at my inn at all. Adrienne was normally calm and collected, and to see her rattled by her feelings made me uncomfortable.

"That thought has crossed my mind. For some reason, though, I think it would be wrong to cancel his reservation. He's...it's like he's *supposed* to be here." She shrugged her shoulders and headed toward the door.

"Hey! Don't just leave me hanging like this, Adrienne." I jumped up, spilling my coffee as I ran after her.

"Hayden, I'm tired, and I need to lie down now."

I knew it was futile to go after her. When Adrienne was finished talking, she was finished, and there was no persuading her otherwise. Sometimes her gift was more like a curse; often her only escape was sleep.

I thought my aunt loved me when she left me this inn in her will. Now I know it was a cruel repayment for the time I threw the cat on her when she was sleeping. Well hell—she was snoring!

Ah, but I digress. I suppose I should stop right here and go back to the beginning. None of this strange tale will make sense unless I explain how the blue blazes I got here in the first place, with *here* being one of the most beautiful Bahamian islands in the Eastern Caribbean. My own little paradise, right? Think again!

Okay, so life back home wasn't that great either. I was living in New Orleans when my aunt died. A month after her passing, her lawyer informed me that she had left me her half of the inn. The other half was still owned by her business partner, Adrienne. I was tickled pink to be part proprietor of an inn in the Bahamas, mainly because it got my ass out of the country before—well, let me explain that part.

I was the not-so-proud owner of a lawn and landscaping business. I did well since it was nearly summer year-round in Louisiana. Hell, even when it was cold there was yard work to be done. It paid the bills and kept me in shape. Simple, stress free, great tan—what more could a girl ask for?

My love life, however, was a disaster. My girlfriend had dumped me for a woman who I thought looked like a Saints linebacker. I gave that woman the best year and a half of my life, and she did this to me. Not to mention she took half my wardrobe and most of my CD collection with her when she left. That part really hurt.

So I cooked up a little scheme. I quietly sold my business to one of my employees, terminated the lease on my apartment, and shipped everything I owned to Cat Island in the Bahamas. Then I paid my ex a visit. Well, not exactly a visit.

It was no surprise to find Carla's car at the gym on any given day since she and her linebacker girlfriend were both addicted to working out. That gym was, of course, where she had met the brute she left me for. What was especially sweet, though, was that Carla always left her car unlocked, a habit I continually fussed at her about to no avail.

An hour before I departed for Cat Island, I dropped by the ol' gym for one last visit. I had spent the entire day before my flight trailing after the neighbor's cat with a Ziploc bag. Yes, I know it was over the top, but Carla deserved the best.

With a bag full of cat turds, I casually walked up to the white Lexus—unlocked, just as I expected. When I was sure no one was around, I gently emptied the contents of said bag beneath the leather-clad driver's seat. The temperature was already ninety-eight degrees. It wouldn't take long for the reeking essence of kitty waste to fill Carla's precious Lexus.

Now I know what I did was disgusting and childish, but the woman broke my heart. Not to mention she was in possession of my entire Melissa Etheridge collection. That alone was grounds enough.

Needless to say, as I waited to board my plane I got a phone call. Carla's voice screeched out so loudly that a dog in a pet carrier several feet from where I sat began to howl. I sat and listened to her tirade with an ear-to-ear grin plastered on my face. Then she put the ox on the phone, who promptly delivered a graphically detailed explanation of just how easily my lungs were going to be ripped out through my nose.

Oh, did I get cocky! I mouthed off so explicitly that half the airport stopped and stared, and I ended by saying, "You know where I live, bitch." They were probably halfway to my old apartment while I was singing that little ditty about *puttin' de lime in de coconut* and catching my first glimpse of the Caribbean from several thousand feet above. Needless to say, going home was not an option. I was in it for the long haul.

Aunt Gloria, God rest her soul, took a liking to me for some unknown reason. After I graduated from high school, she moved to Cat Island and remained there until she died. My dad's sister was her own woman; regardless of what anyone said, she did her own thing. I suppose that's why she liked me—she saw a little of herself in her only niece.

I was rather fond of my headstrong aunt as well. I corresponded with her behind my dad's back all through my high school years, writing her letters and sending her pictures. When I went to college, I sometimes called her on weekends, but, I'm ashamed to admit, I didn't keep in touch nearly enough.

At sixty-seven she died of a massive heart attack and was buried on the island a month before I even knew she had passed. I suppose the word *strained* is an understatement when it comes to describing her relationship with her brother, my father. Dad out-and-out despised her, and she did not give a rat's ass what he thought. She considered that his problem.

The trouble started when she decided to come out and tell the family she was gay. My dad dropped her like a hot rock. He proclaimed that no Tate had ever been a homosexual and she was no longer a member of his family. When he found out about me, it made him hate her even more, as though our shared sexual orientation emanated from some sort of contagious disease. To make matters worse, when my other aunt, Dad's sister Maxine, had passed away she left every red cent (and a healthy sum of money it was) to her baby sister Gloria. And since Dad was, in Gloria's opinion, a first-class butthole, he never saw a penny from her either. And because my brother is very much like my dad, Aunt Gloria passed all her wealth on to her niece—that would me—the one on the airplane grinning like the Cheshire cat headed for Cat Island.

Now, let's move on to the rest of the story. It seems that I will be paying for my harsh treatment of Carla and her bulbous-headed girlfriend for a long time. Vengeance is a bad thing, or so I am learning. The hard way.

On the plane ride over, I had imagined myself kicked back in a hammock sipping a fruity drink with a little twirling umbrella. I had planned to spend most of my days doing just that. However, when I arrived on the island, I quickly learned that was not to be. Cat Island is nothing like Nassau, with its resorts and casinos. Apparently, my aunt loved her solitude, because when I got off the stump jumper of a plane they flew me over in, I felt like I'd stepped through a portal in the Bermuda triangle and landed in another dimension.

As I stood alone on the tarmac, a dilapidated old Jeep roared up next to me. A man, who I swear was a pirate, lumbered out and started toward me. I felt like Buckwheat from the *Little Rascals* praying, "Feets don't fail me now!" I spun in a circle looking for a place to run. That's when I realized I was surrounded by—well, nothing.

The airstrip was nothing more than a long strip of pot-holed asphalt spread smack dab in the middle of nowhere. Both sides of the strip were covered with brambles and bushes; an occasional palm tree swayed in the afternoon breeze. That same breeze blew my long, curly hair over my face, obscuring it from view, and I was glad. I didn't want the pirate to see the panic on my face.

"Hayden Tate?" the pirate barked, causing me to jump. Did I mention he came complete with an eye patch? I stood there like a deer caught in headlights.

"Yes, sir," I responded in a croaky whisper. Apparently my voice had gone into hiding without me.

The big, smelly, hairy man simply walked up, took my bag, threw it into the Jeep, and climbed behind the wheel. My knees felt like jelly as I walked over and climbed in as well. I stole a quick glance over at the burly man as he shifted the vehicle into gear and drove us up a narrow dirt path that eventually connected to the main road. This was a man you would not want to meet in a dark alley. In fact, you would not want to meet him, period.

All he said during the hour-long trip to the inn was, "Name's Hank. Adrienne sent me to fetch you."

I learned a crucial lesson during that ride: somewhere there was a hole in the earth that reached all the way into the deepest part of hell, and rising unimpeded from that hole were all manner of insects that now dwelled on Cat Island. I quickly came to understand why Hank was so quiet—if you opened your mouth, dinner was served.

Huge green insects splattered the windshield as he drove. Dismembered legs and various body parts often sprayed over onto us, and I was nearly blinded when one of their grotesque heads flew into my eye. Bug parts matted in Hank's long, scraggly beard, yet he did not flinch or make any attempt to rid himself of the gory mess. I tried to wipe the insect carnage from my mind by taking in a little of the scenery.

I had been to Nassau a few times while in college, but this place was nothing like that. There were no high-rise resorts, no casinos, no freaking Starbucks! The terrain was beautiful, though, and I was awed by the tropical plant life. As we cruised down the coast highway, occasional clearings in the brush allowed a view of the crystal-clear water that surrounded the island.

When we arrived at the inn, the sun was just setting. I had to admit that the view was breathtaking; however, I did not dare breathe through my mouth for fear of what might fly in. Hank grunted. I took that as a signal that I was supposed to follow him. He led me into an open-air bar and told me to wait there, and of course, I obeyed. He took my bag and disappeared. I hoped that he was taking it to my room, but, if he showed up the following morning with a new Victoria's Secret eye patch, I wasn't saying shit about it.

I sat down in one of the chairs in the little bar and was amazed at how comfortable it was. Had I not been terrified of what the pirate was doing with my luggage, I might have drifted off to sleep in the tranquility of the place. Matter of fact,

I thought I had fallen asleep because an apparition out of a dream approached me.

She was tall, and I had to look straight up to see the most beautiful green eyes I'd ever had the pleasure of gazing into. Her long auburn hair lifted gently in the Caribbean breeze and fluttered around her face in wisps that accentuated the natural red highlights. A simple floral dress hugged her shapely, tanned body. The sight of this gorgeous, barefoot creature made me want to purr.

I have a thing for tall women. I am 5'7", and it is rare to find a woman that I have to look up to. That hair! Oh, how I longed to run my fingers through those flowing, silky locks. Green eyes are also a weakness of mine. I had always wanted green or even blue eyes, but alas, I was tagged with a pair that couldn't make up their mind. At times they were grayish blue, then depending on my mood, greenish blue.

"Welcome to Cat Island, Hayden." Her voice was as beautiful as she was. "How was your trip?" she asked, staring down at me with an angelic expression.

I simply sat and stared like a moron. I think for a second I actually did purr. I couldn't say a word, and I had begun to wonder if I really had drifted off to sleep—that is until a mosquito the size of a 747 speared me on the arm, bringing me back to consciousness.

"Forgive me," I stammered. I stood and awkwardly thrust out a hand for her to shake. When she took my hand into hers, I thought I would melt. My aunt really did love me!

"I'm Adrienne. It's a pleasure to finally meet you," she said with a sweet smile. I could hear my brain slamming on the brakes and skidding to a halt. This woman was my aunt's business partner? I had always assumed that they were lovers as well. Suddenly, I had a newfound respect for my aunt, the little scamp!

"Your aunt and I were never lovers. I thought of her as a mother. She was very dear to me," she snapped.

"Oh, I didn't mean to—" I put my hand to my mouth. Often I stick my foot in there. "Wait a minute. I didn't say...I mean I didn't—"

"You didn't have to." She raised a single brow at me.

Hell. Am I that easy to read? I'm tired—that's it. None of this is making sense right now.

"Look, I'm sorry if I said something to offend you." *Or did I?* I wondered. "I suppose I was just expecting you to be my aunt's age. Not to imply I think you're old. You look to be in your thirties, which is a good thing...I think I'll shut up now."

Adrienne's brow relaxed. "No need to apologize, Hayden. You must be tired from the trip, and I know you probably want to see your new home. I'll show you to your cottage now if you like."

"Yes, I'd like that very much." I pulled one of the hell bugs from my hair. "A shower and a change of clothes might make me feel human again."

"Very well then, please follow me." And follow her I did. If my eyes hadn't been glued to her butt for most of the walk, I might have been able to better appreciate the beautiful courtyard that was the centerpiece of the guest cottages. She led me down a narrow cobblestone path to two cottages that sat secluded from the rest. I was especially happy to note that hers was next to mine.

I was unable to tell exactly what the interior of my cottage looked like because it was filled from floor to ceiling with boxes of my belongings. After a long shower, I felt much better. I peered at my reflection in the mirror—a stark contrast to Adrienne—but grateful my hair was brown again and no longer decorated with bug guts. My fair complexion was still marred with red splotches where bugs had smacked me in the face and neck. First impressions are always the most lasting, and I inwardly cringed, wondering what Adrienne must have thought when her new partner looked like she had been dragged face first across the island.

I cannot deny that my physical attraction to Adrienne was immediate, and I wondered if she found me appealing at all.

Although I'd often been told I was pretty, in Adrienne's presence I felt indescribably plain. And while I considered myself athletic, I still managed to keep my feminine qualities. But I made it a habit not to wear too much makeup, if I wore any at all. Today, however, I put some paint on the old barn, chastising myself for dolling up for the mysterious woman I had just met. Taking a last-minute peek in the mirror, I decided to let my hair hang loose down my back. I topped the look off with a little lipstick, making my already full lips look kissable. Or at least I thought so. Satisfied with the result, I decided to put some clothes on because showing up naked to dinner might not be a good idea.

Once I was dressed, I decided to go in search of two things: Miss tall, dark, and mysterious—and food. I was famished. I found Adrienne in the little bar where we'd first met. She greeted me and led me into the dining room, which I quickly decided that I did not like. It was a small, intimate setting with a huge round table where, I assumed, all the guests dined together. Not being a people person, I was instantly put off by the idea of sharing meals with a table full of strangers.

Adrienne and I sat alone at the big table as a heavyset black woman brought out platter upon platter of beautifully arranged food—but every single dish she presented was some variation of conch. I have never been a great lover of seafood, but my first experience with a conch was unforgettable. The taste and smell and texture of that first bite turned my stomach. And while I managed to discreetly choke it down, there was no way I was going to eat a conch anything ever again. Instead, I filled my empty stomach with salad, bread, and fruit.

After dinner, the same woman emerged from the kitchen to clear away the dishes before returning with a steaming pot of coffee. Adrienne had been mostly quiet during the meal. She had answered all of my questions about the locals and the island itself, choosing to wait until after dinner to discuss the inn.

"Your aunt had a simple way of running things around here. Unlike the rest of the inns and hotels, we book all of our guests for a two-week stay. The following week there are no guests, and we make any needed repairs She wanted it to be similar to the way a cruise ship operates, with a certain number of guests who stay for an all-inclusive two-week vacation."

While Gloria's Inn catered to gay and lesbian couples, they did not turn anyone away as long as they respected the other guests. Adrienne went on to explain that they employed two porters who doubled as tour guides.

"So, you mean to say that dear old Hank doesn't greet the guests?"

"No, he's our handyman. The porters are only here when we have guests. The cleaning and cooking staff works the same way with the exception of Iris, who is the full-time cook."

"When you say repairs, what exactly does that entail? Do the guests get rowdy?" I asked with concern.

"No, not at all," Adrienne replied. "The grounds are extensive and require a good deal of upkeep. And each cottage has a thatched roof, as I am sure you must have noticed. They have to be maintained as well."

"Hank does all of that work by himself?"

Adrienne smiled. It was a smile that said, "You're not going to like this part."

"Your aunt and I, along with Hank, did most of the repairs. She told me that you are quite good with your hands and manual labor is something that you excel at." She cocked her brow suggestively before continuing. "Since you were in the landscaping business, I'm sure you will adapt very easily."

"Okay, there's the problem. We own this place. Why can't we simply hire people to do that?" One corner of Adrienne's mouth twitched slightly, and then I heard that sigh of exasperation. Right before my eyes, I watched my beachcomber, bum-in-the-sun dreams sink like the Titanic.

"Hayden, it takes money to operate this place. We have to cut corners everywhere we can."

"My aunt was loaded. Why on earth would we need to cut corners?" I felt compelled to jump up and shout, "Show me the money!" There was that smile again. It made the hair on the back of my neck rise. I wanted to stuff my fingers in my ears because I knew I was most certainly not going to like what I was about to hear.

"Your aunt was a very benevolent woman, Hayden, and when she started this inn, she chose to give back to the community that had accepted her so lovingly by donating her money to the local medical clinic. And to the little schools here. Bottom line, she was not *loaded*, as you so colorfully describe it, when she died. This inn is all she owned."

Okay, that cinched it; my aunt did indeed hate me. I actually started to entertain the idea of going back to New Orleans and letting the linebacker beat me to a pulp. With a pirate skulking around, bugs the size of crop dusters, and the realization that I would be a working innkeeper, an ass whipping didn't sound half bad.

Then I really screwed up. I looked into that dazzling set of eyes, and I thought *what the hell, I'll give it a try*. If things didn't work out, I could look forward to being eaten alive by some island creature, and no, I did not mean the gorgeous woman sitting next to me.

After Adrienne finished ruining my night with more details about the inn, I decided to retire to my cottage with a bottle of rum. It took me a while, but I finally confirmed that I did in fact have a bed—and not one of those little Gilligan hammocks—under all the boxes. I found a place to sit down, opened the rum, and lit up a cigarette. I followed each drag on the cigarette with a swig straight from the bottle—and pondered my fate.

In another week, a new group of guests would be arriving, and I would be expected to help serve and entertain. I hadn't even seen the place in the daylight. Last but not least, I could have sworn that my business partner could read my mind, which freaked me out and just plain pissed me off. Did I mention the bugs and that pirate guy?

I woke up the following morning to what surely was an entire flock of birds squawking and pecking at the thatched roof on my cottage. In addition, I had drunk a quarter of the bottle of rum, and my lightweight ass had passed out on a box instead of the bed. There wasn't a spot on my body that didn't ache, including my toenails.

A soft knock at my door prompted me to move. I opened the door, squinting painfully in the morning light. Adrienne stood there looking radiant and refreshed, which would have pissed me off if it hadn't been for those damned beautiful eyes staring at me.

"I thought you might need this." She presented a tray that held toast, fruit, and a pitcher of iced tea.

I can be very polite when I want to be, but right then I didn't want to be. "Were you reading my mind again?" I asked snidely.

"Actually, no. I saw you swipe the bottle of rum from the bar last night. Your aunt usually passed out after two drinks, and since you are from her bloodline I figured you would do the same." I didn't miss that little smirky grin of hers when she glanced past me to the nearly full bottle of rum that had rolled against a box. I stepped aside to let her in—she was still holding the tray, after all. She looked around for a moment and selected the very box that I had used for a bed to set the tray on. Two glasses. I assumed she intended to visit. I offered her a box seat and poured us each a glass of tea.

After I drank two glasses, my mouth started to feel normal again. My head felt a little better too, but goodness knows what I must have looked like. I simply didn't have the strength yet to go into the bathroom, so I decided that I could at least try to be polite.

"I'm sorry about the mind-reading remark, Adrienne. Not being a morning person or a drinker, I guess I woke up on the wrong side of the box—um, bed."

"I won't take up much of your time." She sipped her tea. "I just wanted to ask you not to make any rash decisions about this place. It's obviously not what you thought it would be, but given a little time, you'll come to love it, I'm sure. You seem to be much like your aunt, and she grew to love this island, its people, and the inn very dearly. That's why she passed it on to you. Just give it a chance, Hayden, please."

Before I knew what I was doing, I was agreeing to do just that—give this place a chance. She smiled and stood to leave. "Your aunt told me that you are a very neat and orderly person, so I imagine that you will want to get your things in order here before you do anything else. Would you like me to stay and help?"

It's not easy to be sociable and make small talk with a hangover. I declined her offer and agreed to meet with her later that afternoon to discuss preparations for the incoming group of guests.

After three solid hours of sorting and putting things away, my cottage looked entirely different and felt more like home. It was slightly bigger than the guest cottages, and there was more than enough room to store all of my belongings neatly away. I was especially pleased to find a built-in desk and bookshelf.

I applauded my decision to purchase a laptop; anything bigger would have dominated the entire desk. I filled the bookshelves with my books and DVD collection. Fortunately, my DVD and CD players fit nicely into the armoire that was used to conceal the TV.

Once I had everything the way I wanted, I showered and got dressed. I arrived a little late for lunch, so I nibbled on a roll and some fruit. At this rate, I would be skinny as a rail in no time. I needed some food—real food, not the conch stuff they kept trying to ram down my throat. That would be my first order of business when I caught up with Adrienne.

CHAPTER TWO

I found Adrienne stretched out on a chaise in the open-air bar reading a book. When I sat in one of the chairs near her and lit up my after-lunch cigarette, she lowered the book to reveal only her eyes and one arched eyebrow. Instinctively, I knew the rest of her face held a grimace. Her eyes darted to the offending smoke I held in my hand.

"Before you start, let me say one thing. This is a bar, and it's open and well ventilated. Second, yes, I know and I agree— it is a disgusting habit, and I go to great lengths for my clothes and breath not to smell like it. Third, and most important, right now this is the only thing keeping me sane. So tread lightly."

"That was three things, but consider the point taken." Adrienne marked her place in the book and set it down. "Are you ready to be indoctrinated into the inn business?"

"As ready as I will ever be," I sighed.

"Good. Wait here, and I'll be right back."

I couldn't resist the temptation of staring at her lovely backside as she walked away; silently, I scolded myself for being such a pig. When she returned, she was carrying two tremendous ledgers. My heart sank. Obviously, they were still in the dark ages and had not upgraded to a computer.

After a couple of hours of poring through pages of neatly printed figures, I had to admit that even though the books were kept the old-fashioned way, it was easy to see how the finances were managed. They were remarkably accurate, a state I attributed to Adrienne alone since my aunt had never been known for maintaining a budget, much less for keeping records.

I had had just about as much as I could stand, and my eyes began to roll up in my head. Fortunately, Adrienne received a phone call that was going to take a little while. And since I wanted to get better acquainted with my new surroundings, I left her a note explaining that I was going on a little walk, then grabbed a banana from the fruit bowl and went on my merry way.

I discovered that the bar was the main receiving area. It was open on three sides, with the kitchen and dining area attached at the rear. During inclement weather, large shades could be rolled down to keep the furniture dry.

The bar and most of the grounds lay under a sheltering canopy of palm trees and banana plants that enhanced the inn's tropical appeal. The dense shade, coupled with the constant breeze, negated the need for air-conditioning. All I could hear were the sounds of nature and the pounding surf on the beach. I walked to the rear of the bar to a courtyard where a fountain with trickling water added a soothing effect to the already tranquil atmosphere.

I slipped my sandals off so I could feel the cool stone under my feet as I walked around admiring the elegantly landscaped yard. Narrow cobblestone paths branched out toward each of the guest cottages that ringed the courtyard.

The inn was nestled on a bluff that overlooked blue Caribbean waters; a tropical forest framed the other three sides. I marveled at the lush plant life that flourished on the island, recognizing numerous varieties that people paid top dollar for back in the States—and they just grew wild here.

I wandered down a cobblestone path that was completely shaded by banana plants and tropical foliage; the farther I went into the tunnel of shadows, the more it seemed that the path wasn't leading anywhere in particular, just away from the cottages. A few minutes later, shafts of light sawed through the broad leaves overhead and cut across the path and the sound of crashing waves got louder. I stepped into the full light of the open bluff and the spectacular, unspoiled view of the coastline took my breath away. Crystalline waters beckoned me, and I had to fight the urge to strip and run down the staircase to the water.

I will admit that upon arrival, I was disappointed to find the island so rural. I was expecting a resort atmosphere with calypso music, beauty spas, and a wait staff dressed in pristine white uniforms catering to my every whim. The reality of the place, however, was completely opposite; yet, I felt a sense of contentment in spite of my disappointment. No doubt it would take me a while to adjust to the slower pace and the antiquated way of doing things, but there was no one back home for me to miss. Just my way of life that I'd grown tired of.

I took a deep breath, filled my lungs with sea air, and walked about fifty yards down the sugar-white beach. Refreshed and exhilarated, I started the short hike back to the inn. I had taken just two steps when I saw it. My body reacted instantly, but it took my brain a second longer to register what my eyes saw and why I was moving so fast. As I leapt into a small tree, I let out a high-pitched girl scream so shrill that it hurt my own ears. The small, scrubby tree bowed under my weight, nearly dropping me onto the snake I was trying to escape from.

Then I saw Adrienne, there at the head of the trail, doubled over laughing. Not just a mere belly laugh, either; the hateful heifer was wheezing and gasping for air, she was laughing so hard!

"You're a Louisiana native; surely you've seen a snake before." She wiped the tears from her eyes. Her body still shook with laughter.

The snake, however, was not any more amused at my antics than I was with Adrienne's laughter, and it slithered off into the brush. After I was certain the snake was gone, I attempted to climb out of the tree, but every movement made its wiry limbs sway harder beneath me. I struggled to keep my balance, but the tree flung me to the ground, snagging the bottom of my shirt and stripping me of it as I fell.

I sat there under the tree in nothing but my bra and shorts, trying to figure out what the hell had happened. Adrienne sounded like a wild hyena in heat as she fell to her knees and laughed uncontrollably. *Stupid tropical island, never a coconut around when you need one.* I made do instead with a fantasy coconut that clipped Adrienne just above that eyebrow she constantly arched. That oughta straighten that out.

I wrestled my shirt from the hateful little tree and quickly pulled what was left of it on. Adrienne sat on the ground, still crying with laughter. I walked passed her and muttered, "Thanks for all your help. Be glad it wasn't a coconut tree."

I could still hear her laughter carried on that wretched ocean breeze as I walked red-faced back to my cottage.

Minutes later I heard a knock on my door and a few muffled giggles as I pulled on a new shirt. I opened the door to find a totally unrepentant Adrienne with tears of laughter still on her face. I gave her the most intimidating glare I could muster.

"Sorry," she muttered under her breath. Her face contorted under the strain of trying to keep what little composure she had regained. "I just wanted to make sure you were all right."

"Nothing wounded but my pride," I scowled.

She stood there quietly for a minute. I could tell she was fighting the urge to laugh again. "So, I take it you have a fear of snakes. No one who works here has ever been bitten, nor have any of the guests. They're often more afraid of you than you are of them." She paused, still chuckling. "Although in your case, maybe not." The irritating chuckle evolved into a full-blown howl of laughter. It was more than my ego could handle.

"I'll see you at dinner," I spat, then slammed the door in her face. I could still hear her laughter fading into the distance as she walked away.

There's not much in this world that I hate more than a snake. Living in Louisiana meant living with snakes, and I encountered the vile things on a regular basis while working outside. However, my reaction was always the same: screaming, loss of bladder control, running in stark terror. They have caused me to hurt myself more than a few times during my escape. Fortunately, this time I did manage not to wet my pants, or I would have left the island permanently.

I lit up a cigarette and calmed myself down. If I was to face Adrienne any time soon, I needed to let my temper cool. She was a very beautiful woman, but I think beneath the surface she possessed the ability to seriously kick my ass. Not to mention she was a good bit taller than me. At least I could get in a few good shots to her kneecaps.

I flopped down on the bed, grabbed the remote, and flicked through the channels looking for something to take my mind off my embarrassment. Had I been in Nassau, I would have been in the spa enjoying a massage, letting someone rub the tension from my neck and shoulders. Instead, I lay shut away in a cottage on a bug-infested, shit-for-TV-programming island—stewing in my anger until I drifted off to sleep.

I slept a lot longer than I intended and was awakened by a gentle knock on my door. Adrienne was again standing there when I opened it. She had a bottle of red wine tucked under her arm. This time she was kind enough not to laugh at my earlier misfortune.

"I was hoping we would have dinner in my cottage tonight. There are a few things I would like to go over with you. Iris made spaghetti—conch free since I know you're not fond of it. She'll bring it out in about twenty minutes. Will you join me?"

On the pretense of behaving like a big girl, I graciously accepted her offer, excused myself to go get cleaned up, and arrived at her place as Iris brought in the meal.

"How was your first day on the island, Hayden?" She greeted me warmly, then shot Adrienne a quick grin that did not go unnoticed by me.

"It was very enlightening, Iris," I responded cheerfully.

She smiled and nodded and left us to our dinner. When she closed the door, I hurled Adrienne a vicious look. "Exactly how many people on this island know about my little adventure today?"

Adrienne pulled my chair out and gestured for me to sit down. "Only Iris. She's deathly afraid of snakes too, you know."

I sat down, suddenly not feeling very hungry. Adrienne glanced over at me as she loaded up my salad plate. "I really am sorry if I offended you this afternoon. If you had seen it from my perspective, you would have laughed too. I had just walked out onto the bluff and then you screamed and jumped straight up into that tree. Then when you fell and your shirt got hung up—" She paused, fighting the urge to laugh again. "I'm really sorry. I'm sure it must have scared you half to death. I might have done the same thing had I been in your shoes." She shifted in her chair. "Look, I hate the idea of us getting off on the wrong foot on your first day. Will you forgive me?"

She looked at me pleadingly. I wanted to hang on to my anger, but—those eyes, that voice—I had no choice but to let it go. I tried to think of a way to make pleasant conversation and prove that I had gotten over the earlier incident. "Adrienne, I don't think you have ever told me your last name. What is it?"

"Cangelosi." She did not bother to say more.

"That's Italian, I assume. I'll bet you can cook like a pro," I said, hoping she would open up and tell me more about herself.

She glanced up and smiled. "On the contrary—I can't cook at all. Matter of fact, Iris won't allow me anywhere near the kitchen. I scorched one of her best pans making popcorn once and I've been banned ever since." She chuckled.

"Do you have any siblings?"

"I have one sister, nine years younger. We've never been really close; I suppose it's because we don't have any interests in common."

She then turned the conversation to me. "How do you and your brother get along?"

"We don't," I said with a frown. "He's a lot like my dad, arrogant, proud, and narrow-minded. Everything seems to revolve around money and their standing in the community. I've never been interested in social status. Plus the fact that I'm gay doesn't sit well with them. They consider it an insult to the Tate name."

I had wondered about Adrienne's sexuality since I arrived on the island. I knew my aunt had told her I was gay, but Adrienne never let on. I didn't want to come right out and ask her if she was; I thought that would have been a little rude. No matter how I tried, I could not keep her on the topic long enough to get her to say one way or the other.

As we ate, she explained that Sunday, only a few days away, the guests would arrive. There would be six couples, all women who visited every year. The cottages were already prepared for them, but we had to order supplies from the mainland. We agreed to handle that task the following morning. I asked Adrienne in what capacity I would be dealing with the guests. My obvious displeasure must have shown on my face.

She smiled. "It's not nearly as bad as you're imagining. The porters and wait staff will be here. You and I will simply tend bar and entertain them at meals. It really is like getting together with old friends. You'll find yourself enjoying this place as much as they do."

I was more than a little skeptical. I was the loner type and really on the timid side, especially in a large group of people. I suppose that's why I did so well in the landscaping business. Often it was only me and lots of dirt that didn't talk back.

"I don't mind telling you, Adrienne, I'm a little nervous about all of this entertaining stuff. This may come as a surprise to you, but I'm actually a little on the shy side. It is truly an effort for me to make casual conversation with people I don't know."

"You'll do just fine," she assured me. "I'll be right by your side."

After dinner, we took our wineglasses and retired to the courtyard where I could smoke. We sat in the patio chairs and talked about life on the island. I learned that Adrienne was originally from Florida and had happened upon the island while wandering in her travels. She was one of the first guests to stay at the inn, and after becoming great friends with my aunt she simply never went back.

"Why do you smoke, Hayden?" she asked as I lit another cigarette.

"Well, basically I'm a nervous person. It helps to calm my nerves even though I hate the way a cigarette tastes. You'll always see me drinking something when I smoke." I raised my glass. "Needless to say, this little plan backfires when the drink has alcohol, since the more I smoke the more I drink and the more I drink the more I smoke. I tend to get a little loopy." I set the glass down, already feeling the effects, and leaned back to listen to the surf. It was almost as calming as the cigarette. Then out of the blue, I asked, "Where is my aunt buried?"

Adrienne's face turned solemn. "At a little cemetery within walking distance of the inn. She wanted to be close to the place she loved." Her eyes misted.

My heart broke for her. I could see that she had loved my aunt very deeply and obviously missed her companionship. She sniffed a little before she spoke. "Your aunt was very precious to me. As I have said before, I thought of her as a mother. She was the only person in this world who ever took the time to understand me."

"I'd like to visit her grave since I was unable to attend her funeral. If it's not too painful, would you accompany me tomorrow?" I asked, hoping not to make her cry.

She looked at me and smiled. "Yes, I'd like that very much. I put fresh flowers on her grave each week."

Adrienne walked me back to my cottage and then returned to her own. I had loved my aunt, but I didn't know her as well as Adrienne had. It made me sad to think how it must have broken her heart when my aunt passed from this life. My heart was heavy with the knowledge of what Adrienne lost when I drifted off to sleep that night.

The following morning I woke up about six o'clock. Bless Adrienne, she had arranged for a coffeepot and fresh beans to be placed in my room. I brewed a pot and sat out on the doorstep, enjoying a cup and a smoke. Ah, life's little pleasures.

A rustling in the hibiscus by the end of the steps caught my attention. I was just about to bolt and run, fearing another bout with a snake, when a puny orange tiger-striped tabby cat poked his head out. He didn't look any older than a couple of months. I coaxed the kitten over and listened to him purr as I scratched behind his ears. Adrienne had said that many stray cats roamed the property, sort of like all the Hemingway cats but not as many. Judging by the display of ribs poking out, I figured the little fella was one of the many vagabonds and was in need of a home and food.

I had a stash of peanut butter crackers, which I shared with the little cat. He ate them like there was no tomorrow. When he had his fill, he rolled over on his back and sunned his little striped belly in the morning sun.

I was amused at how his lip seemed to always be curled up over one of his front fangs. It made him look as though he had a perpetual snarl, kind of like a saber-toothed tiger. So, Saber he was dubbed, and on my second day on the island I adopted a cat.

Luckily, my former job had called for casual dress. I had an endless pile of shorts and lightweight shirts perfect for the island climate. I showered and dressed and went off to find more suitable fare for my newly adopted feline. Iris fixed me up with some dry cat food she kept on hand for the strays and two bowls perfect for a kitty. It seemed Iris had a soft spot for cats too.

Adrienne walked up as Saber was discovering his new food bowls. He cast a casual glance and began to chow down. I figured his paws were hollow because I had no idea where he stored all the food he consumed. I made sure he had plenty of fresh water and then accompanied Adrienne to the bar.

I was falling in love with Iris and nearly fell to the floor and kissed her feet when she took control of the table where we were working and laid out before me two different pitchers of fresh island juices, bacon, and sourdough pancakes topped with her homemade raspberry preserves. She did not escape without a heartfelt hug.

As we ate breakfast, Adrienne made a list of the things we would need. I added a couple of boxes of Count Chocula—if I didn't get that stuff soon, somebody was going to get hurt. I listened as she called in our order. Afterward, she explained that it would be delivered by boat within the next two days, weather permitting. I was thrilled. The Count was on his way.

We worked off breakfast by walking up the road to my aunt's grave site, stopping at intervals to gather fresh tropical flowers to lay on the headstone. It seemed rather strange not to call a florist to order an arrangement. But to be able to gather a bouquet from right along the path—I realized that Aunt Gloria would appreciate these all the more since they were offerings directly from the soil of the land she loved.

When we reached the grave, Adrienne politely stood back and allowed me a moment alone. Deep down inside, I hadn't accepted Gloria's death—until now. As I sat in front of the tombstone marking the piece of earth where the dearest person in my life lay buried, reality finally sank in. I could not stop the tears that ran down my cheeks as I mourned.

This woman had obviously touched the lives of her community deeply: mounds of flowers covered her grave site. I had always known that Aunt Gloria was a very open and caring person. It should not have come as a surprise that she was so well loved here.

I stood back and allowed Adrienne her time alone, and as she knelt down to lovingly place her flowers, I wondered if I would be able to fill Aunt Gloria's shoes. I decided at that moment that I wanted to carry on what Gloria had started and silently vowed to continue her commitment—whatever profit the inn made, a portion would still go to supporting this community.

On the walk back, Adrienne and I were both quiet, lost in our own thoughts and emotions. I had been here only a day and a half, yet this place had already begun to change me. I was starting to see why my aunt never desired to leave this place, never cared to return to the land where she was born or to her family.

As we neared the inn, I broke the silence. "So, what else do we need to do in preparation for our guests?" When Adrienne did not readily answer, I decided to make a stab at humor. "If it involves snakes, I'm telling you right now—count me out."

She smiled. That smile was beginning to get to me, but I fought it valiantly by replaying images of her merciless laughter at my expense because I didn't think it would be a good idea to get romantically involved with someone I had to work with so closely. Still, I could not deny the fact that I found her utterly captivating.

"We rest."

"Rest? That's all? I thought you said there's a lot of work to be done in between guests." I was not accustomed to rest.

"Your aunt could have made a fortune by booking guests continually like the other inns do, but she wanted us all to have time for ourselves. She always said, 'What is the use of having all this if you don't make time to enjoy it?' We do all the cleaning, maintenance, and preparations for the next group right after the guests leave. And then for most of the time we have left, we simply rest and relax and enjoy the island."

"How do you plan to spend the rest of the day?"

There was that smile again. "I had planned on getting my snorkeling gear and going down to the beach. Iris usually packs me a lunch, and I spend the day on the beach reading and playing in the water."

"You do this alone?"

"No. A few friends usually join me."

I didn't know why, but my heart sank when she said that. I figured a woman as beautiful as Adrienne would obviously have someone with whom she spent her time, and I didn't want to be a third wheel. I felt another emotion that surprised me: jealousy had reared its ugly head.

"I'd love it if you would join us," she offered politely.

I was about to decline the offer when we were rushed by a group of boys who I figured ranged in age from seven to ten. I watched as she hugged each one. From the looks on their little faces, they obviously adored her.

"Hayden, allow me to introduce my beach buddies." She called each of their names, and one by one, although a little warily, they approached to shake my hand like little gentlemen.

"So, what about it, Hayden? Will you join us?"

All the boys looked at me expectantly, and when I agreed, they jumped around excitedly and swarmed Adrienne.

"She's going! She's going, Miss Adrienne!"

"Okay, fellas, help me get the gear and food down to the beach while Miss Hayden goes up to change."

"Hurry back, Miss Hayden."

"Back in a flash!" I shouted over my shoulder as I loped back to my cottage.

Upon my arrival, I found a dead lizard lying on my doormat. My new feline friend stood triumphantly nearby, eyeing the gift he had cemented our relationship with. He was now the proud owner of a human. I silently prayed that he would not feel the need to bring me any more gifts. I shuddered, thinking the next might very well be a snake.

Once I gathered my things, I cautiously walked back down the narrow path to the bluff, relieved that I had not encountered any creatures of the slimy, snaky variety by the time I reached the clearing.

The sight on the beach warmed my heart. I watched as Adrienne chased the group of little boys up and down the sandy beach in a game of tag. She was absolutely beautiful. Her hair blew free in the breeze, and her tanned skin shone like gold reflecting the sun. She was radiant.

When I made the trek across the beach, the boys grabbed their snorkeling gear and waited patiently as I dug mine out of the bag. Snorkeling was one of my favorite hobbies, and I looked forward to seeing what was beneath those crystal-clear waters.

Adrienne gathered the boys together and made all of them be quiet before she spoke. "You know the rules, gang. Everyone must have a buddy, and we all stay together in a group."

I took that moment to ogle her in a swimsuit. Her tanned legs went on for days. The teal bikini that she sported covered all of the important parts but left little to the imagination. I couldn't wait for her to get into the water because I was sure it would cling to her skin even more. Had I not been in a group of little boys, I might have been tempted to chase her down the beach like a rabid dog.

I watched as the boys paired off. My heart sank when the smallest of the group was left without a partner. I approached him and smiled as sweetly as I knew how, which might have scared him a little. "You're Kevin, right?"

"Yes'm, Miss Hayden." His voice was small and timid.

"Well, Kevin, it seems that I don't have a buddy. Would you mind pairing up with me?"

His face lit up with a smile as he nodded and curled his small hand around my fingers. I looked down into his big brown eyes and could not imagine denying that child anything at that moment. Children had always gotten on my last nerve. They were loud, obnoxious, insufferable little creatures. And what they did not break, they peed on. I knew right then that I had officially gone insane.

As Kevin led me to the water, I glanced over and noticed Adrienne watching us with the most peculiar expression on her face. When she realized that she had been caught staring, she smiled and accompanied her snorkeling buddy into the water.

We moved as a group to a small jetty of rocks. My buddy stayed close to my side, and I often caught those big brown eyes watching me intently. It took me a little while, but I noticed the protectiveness in his actions. This little child was watching over me, making sure I was all right. The little guy made my heart melt.

The coral reef, nestled in shallow water, teemed with sea life. I watched dozens of bright-colored fish, many I had only seen in fish tanks back home, as they darted in and out of the coral. Seeing the reef through a child's eyes, its beauty and simplicity—things we adults take for granted—made this snorkeling trip the best one ever. We spent at least two hours circling the reef, discovering new spectacles at each turn. I found Adrienne studying me more than once with the same peculiar expression.

Hunger eventually had us all scrambling back to shore where Iris's picnic basket awaited us. To my supreme delight, there was no conch; instead, we had ham and turkey sandwiches and fruit for desert.

With our bellies full, Adrienne and I stretched out on the sand and watched the children play in the surf. As I lay there, the thought occurred to me that these children did not care that I glowed like a neon beacon next to their ebony skin. People are people, regardless of color, but even in this day and age, someone was always available to make an issue of their perceived distinctions between the races. It angered me to think that, had we been in the States, two white women in the company of several black children would still seem strange, if not downright improper, to some passersby. I found it refreshing that to these children, I was simply Miss Hayden, the woman who had spent the day playing with them.

As if she were reading my thoughts, Adrienne spoke up. "They are beautiful children, aren't they? They're so innocent and pure; they know nothing of racism, nor do they care what color we are. They simply see people as people, and all they want is someone who will take a genuine interest in them."

One of the boys approached us. "Is it time for our story now, Miss Adrienne?" She smiled and nodded, and all the boys came racing ashore. She pulled a tattered copy of *The Lion, The Witch and the Wardrobe* from her bag and began to read. I watched as each child lay in the warm sand and was transported to Narnia on Adrienne's voice. Before I realized it, I was traveling with them.

Adrienne and I walked together behind the kids as we made our way back to the inn. We watched them as they played together on the walk and explored the same things they must have seen a million times. I was wary when we started up the narrow path and surprised myself by walking ahead, making sure there were no slimy snakes on the trail.

We arrived at the inn as Iris was serving food on the patio tables in the courtyard. Adrienne, the children, and I dined on fried chicken, mashed potatoes, and peas. After everyone had eaten their fill, Adrienne and I both hugged and kissed each child before they left for home. I couldn't help but wonder if I had lost my mind; I had actually enjoyed the company of a bunch of rowdy little boys.

I was beat when I got back to the cottage, so I showered and relaxed in front of the television for a while. My mind kept going back to the woman I had spent the day with. I wondered what she was doing and hoped she was as tired as I was so I wouldn't feel like such a wimp.

I lay in bed admiring my new home. It wasn't the posh place I expected, but its simplicity held a unique charm. I had put my own comforter set on my bed to give the place a more homelike atmosphere. The nautical pattern meshed nicely with the tropical décor. The floor was made of stone tablets with decorative mosaic inlays. I loved the way it felt, cool against my feet. Aside from the garden tub in my bathroom, my favorite feature was the floor-to-ceiling screened windows that were positioned to allow the Caribbean breeze to blow unhindered through my room.

I heard a familiar scratching at the door and grinned. I knew it was Saber, back to fill his belly. He strolled in as I opened the door and gave me a meow as if saying hello. He went straight to his food and filled up his hollow legs.

When I turned the lights out, he jumped on the bed and curled up against me. He kicked his purr motor into high gear, and soon we were both asleep. Sometime during the night, he grew restless and slapped the clock by my bed onto the floor. When I got up he went straight to the door to be let out, thus beginning the pattern for our nights to come.

CHAPTER THREE

I thought I was becoming ill the next day when I got up at six-thirty in the morning all by myself, no alarm clock, nothing. I pressed the back of my hand to my forehead to check for fever, confirming what I already knew. I was perfectly healthy. I was simply losing my mind.

Actually enjoying the company of kids, a desire to better the community, adopting strays—yep, I was losing it. It had to be something in that iced tea they were always offering me. Or worse, maybe I was being brainwashed in my sleep. I could just picture the lot of them gathered around my cottage at night, blowing into those damn conch shells and chanting nice words over and over. This was a nightmare!

I got up and stumbled over to the coffeepot. Once I had it brewing, I went into the bathroom to look into the mirror and see if I was still me. I looked at the image staring back at me and noticed some subtle changes. I actually looked relaxed. I stared at myself as I brushed my teeth. Something was happening to me, and what scared me the most was that I kind of liked it.

I showered, dressed, poured myself a cup of coffee, and was ready to face the day by seven o'clock. When I opened the door to sit on the step, Saber met me with an irritated meow. Of course, he shot past me and headed straight for his food. He joined me later as I sat enjoying my cigarette and coffee. I absently stroked his fur, still feeling a sense of solitude even in his presence, as the tropical forest came alive all around me. I breathed in the fresh scent of the ocean breeze. Then it hit me. The most offensive odor I think I had ever smelled. I looked down at the orange kitten. "Saber, how could you? I had my mouth open and was drinking my coffee!" The odor didn't pass. Perhaps it was not coming *out* of the cat but was *on* the cat. I picked up the little ball of fur and gave him a sniff. I gagged as I set him back down. He smelled as though he had wallowed in something that had been dead for a week in the hot sun. "Saber, you're not going to like this. It's bath time."

I ran a little water in the bathroom sink and set one of my best-smelling shampoos next to it. Then I went in search of Mr. Stinky. Everything was going fine, the purr motor was on full blast, he was looking up at me with little orange eyes of love, and then I stuck him in the water.

A noise came out of that cat that made me want to run into the woods screaming. I stood my ground, though, and did my best to keep his little body in the water as I reached for the shampoo. I managed to get him all soaped up; he even seemed to relax a little as I rubbed the shampoo into his fur. However, when it came time to rinse him, he made that noise again and I almost gave up.

I wrapped the little pissed-off feline in a towel and dried him as best I could. I did wonder if I had shrunk him when I pulled him from the towel. When I turned the hair dryer on to fluff him a bit, he shot out of my hands like a rocket, and I swear if the door had not already been open he would have ripped a cat-shaped hole in it.

I cleaned the bathroom sink and mopped up all the water with a towel, all the while trying to imagine what that cat had gotten into to make him smell that bad. There was no way he was getting back in bed with me when he smelled like road kill.

My stomach sounded like I had a family of bears living in it. Time to see what dear Iris had cooked up for breakfast. She met me in the dining room doorway and informed me that

Adrienne was in the bar waiting on me. I joined her and we ate our blueberry waffles. Yes, Iris had definitely won my heart.

Adrienne and I ate in comfortable silence. I was so full that I debated going back to bed. But Adrienne invited me to take a morning walk, and I readily accepted. This time we went the opposite direction from the graveyard so I could see a little more of the scenery.

We passed a small pineapple farm neighboring the inn. I watched as the family that owned it made their way through the field gathering the ripe fruit by hand and loading their harvest onto a wooden cart. They all smiled and waved as we walked by. This way of life was utterly foreign to me, yet I felt at home.

Adrienne was proving to be a quiet, introspective woman. She didn't have a whole lot to say in the way of casual conversation. If I wanted to have a conversation with her, I would have to ask her questions and pull the information out of her.

"So, tell me about the arriving guests. I assume you know them pretty well since they come here regularly," I said as I kicked rocks up the dirt road.

"Well, there are six couples. One pair is not an actual couple, however; they're together as friends. They came last year, but they both had mates then. They're all close friends who live in the same city, and once a year they get together and come here for a break. They really are a lot of fun; your aunt and I spent a good deal of time with them talking and playing cards. This place really comes alive when they're here."

She suddenly stopped walking and glanced at me for a second. "Calvin is ahead of schedule and will be here in a couple of hours. We should go back to the inn." She turned and started walking briskly.

I ran and half skipped, trying to keep up with her long stride. Finally, when I thought I would pass out, I grabbed her by the arm. "Can we slow it down a bit before I'm facedown in the dirt?" I asked, gasping for breath.

She looked a little surprised, and then I realized I was still holding her arm. "Who is Calvin?" I asked in confusion as I let her go.

"Calvin is the guy that runs the supply boat. He's ahead of schedule and is coming today instead of tomorrow." She ran her fingers through her hair nervously as her eyes darted back and forth, obviously uncomfortable about something. Then it hit me like a lightening bolt. She must have something going on with Calvin to be acting so strangely.

Even though I knew it would not be wise to get involved with Adrienne, I was a little disappointed that I would never get the chance. It was so depressing to meet a gorgeous woman only to find out she was batting for the other team, unless Calvin was a woman. Ah well, like I had a shot anyway.

I gave her a weak smile, and we continued walking. I had not realized how far we had gone; the walk seemed much longer on the way back. I'm sure it had a lot to do with giraffe woman's stride. It was a struggle to keep up with her.

I got nosey and decided to get the whole scoop. I tried to be funny, which was my first mistake. "Wow, Calvin must be something special to make you scramble like this."

She smiled but didn't offer any info; nor did she slow her pace.

"Please remind me why we walked out this far if he was coming so soon to make a delivery?"

"It wasn't until we got out here that I knew he was coming this soon."

I didn't remember her talking on a cell phone. Matter of fact, I couldn't get a signal on mine at all. I decided to push the issue.

"Okay, how did you know he was early?" I asked as I grabbed her arm again, pulling her to a stop.

She gave me a look that gave me the chills. I couldn't tell what was hiding behind her eyes. For a moment it looked like anger, but I couldn't be sure. I let go of her arm and waited for her answer.

"I don't know how to explain this to you, Hayden." She sighed. "And this will make no sense to you, but sometimes...sometimes I just know things."

We began to walk again, but this time she slowed her pace a bit. Finally I said, "No, it really doesn't make sense. What do you mean you know things? Are you a mind reader?"

She ran her hand through her hair again, apparently a nervous habit that I have to admit I found completely sexy. I made a mental note to make her more nervous in the future.

"No, I can't read minds. I don't really know how it happens or where it comes from; I've given up on finding out. It comes just like a thought, and I simply know."

"Have you ever been wrong?"

"When I was younger I often misinterpreted things, but now that I'm older it's more distinct."

This sounded like something from a cheesy sci-fi flick. I was having a hard time believing her, and naturally the ass in me had to come out. "Please tell me you didn't read my mind last night when I was fantasizing about you covered in whipped cream." I chuckled. Sometimes I amuse myself. She, however, was not amused in the least.

"Hayden, I am not one of those phonies you see on TV, and I do not consider myself a physic. I'm not asking you to believe anything. I simply answered your question!" This time there was anger in her eyes, and, I am ashamed to say, pain.

"Look, I'm sorry. I've just never believed in anything like that, and you caught me a little off guard. I'm sorry if I offended you." I didn't know why I was apologizing; I still thought she was off her rocker.

"Don't be sorry. I'm used to it," she said, waving me off just as we arrived at the inn. Without another word, she walked off toward her cottage. Instinctively, I knew it best not to follow.

"Hayden?" I turned to see Iris standing at the bar holding the phone out to me. I walked over and took it from her, wondering who would be calling me here.

An unfamiliar male voice spoke when I answered. "Hi, Hayden, this is Calvin. I haven't been able to reach Hank, and I have a load of supplies. Would you or Adrienne mind meeting me at the dock?"

I was a little taken aback that Adrienne was right about Calvin, but I was still skeptical. I agreed to meet Calvin at the dock within the hour. Iris gave me directions and I took the van, thrilled with the prospect of driving something enclosed this time. My last ride across the island with Hank still gave me the chills.

I drove down to Warren Harbor and pulled as close to the dock as I could. I hopped out of the van and walked down the dock to a dilapidated boat pulling into the slip. A short, stocky, balding man called out to me as I approached. He looked like a tanned Mr. Clean with a goatee.

"Are you Hayden Tate?"

"That depends on whether or not you have Count Chocula on board," I said with a grin.

He laughed. "I sure do. Could you give me a hand and grab the stern line?" He tossed me a rope. I did my best to tie the line correctly. I didn't want him drifting off until I got my cereal.

After the boat was secured to the dock, we began the laborious task of loading the large boxes of supplies into the van. He explained that normally Hank came out to meet him and apologized for needing my help. I accepted his apology; however, I was more pleased with the shiny gold explanation glinting from around his ring finger.

When we finished the load, both of us were sweating like mules and he smelled like one. I accepted his invitation to have a soda and waited for him on the stern, cooling in the breeze while he fetched two Cokes. I was most pleased to see the pictures he brought out too—pictures of his wife and kids, one a newborn. Calvin was obviously a happily married man, judging by how he prattled on about the family. Yes, I was definitely thrilled to see those family photos.

I had a spring in my step as I walked up the dock to the van. Calvin was married, and that meant that he and Adrienne were not an item. Maybe, just maybe, Adrienne was not batting for the other team. Although by that point, I was convinced that she was insane.

I didn't think there would ever be a time that I thought I would be happy to see Hank, but that day was the exception. After I backed the van into the little loading zone behind the inn, he helped unload while I helped Iris put up the kitchen supplies. In return, she gave me a special spot in her pantry for my cereal.

Hank carried the heavier boxes of liquor to the bar, but that was about as far as he got. Unpacking them must not have been in his contract. When I got back to the bar, he was nowhere in sight; frankly, I wasn't about to complain.

I was busy unloading the boxes and stocking the liquor behind the bar when Iris placed a turkey sandwich in front of me. I definitely loved that woman. Adrienne was on my mind as I sat behind the bar eating my sandwich, half tempted to fix myself a rum and Coke. I was pouring myself a Coke when Adrienne walked into the bar and without a word picked up a book off one of the chaise lounges. She was about to walk out when she turned suddenly and gave me an icy glare. "You may want to stay right there by the phone, your mother will be calling." Then she walked out before I could say a word.

Not two minutes later the phone rang. It scared me so badly I nearly fell off the bar stool, and what was left of my sandwich splatted on the floor. I don't know why, but I was surprised to hear my mom's voice on the phone. I reached under the bar, quickly deciding to have that rum after all.

"Hayden, your father is furious that you went to that inn. He will not allow me to mention your name in this house, absolutely forbids it. Now tell me, have you put it on the market yet? How much do you think it will bring?" She rattled off a stream of questions while I sipped my drink, and when I felt my eyes go into a roll, I started listening to the tune jingling around in my brain—some old song I'd heard, something about *drinkin' rum and Coca-Cola*. I lit a cigarette somewhere around the middle of the song, and of course she heard the lighter click and launched into a whole new tirade that any preacher would have been proud of.

When she finally did stop to catch a breath, after one more order for me to "sell that cesspool," I took great pleasure informing her that I had no plans to sell the inn, and furthermore, that I was happy on Cat Island and had every intention of staying on. That really set her off. I eased the phone down on the bar and enjoyed my drink. Even though I could still hear her ranting, I was blissfully ignorant of exactly what she was saying until "Hayden Marie Tate, you answer me!" blasted over the line. I grabbed the phone again.

"Mom—"

"What on earth are you doing that you can't answer your own mother?"

Recovering quickly, I blurted out that I had some pressing matters to attend to and hung up. I spied a chaise lounge in a shady corner of the bar and decided to claim it for my own. I stretched out and sipped my drink, thinking about my chat with Adrienne. I must have drifted off to sleep because the next thing I knew, Iris was gently shaking me. Dinner would be served in the dining room in ten minutes. I wasn't fit to share airspace with after my morning workout on the dock, so I hurried back to my cottage for a quick shower. I noticed that Saber had not returned since the bath episode that morning. I silently scolded myself for pissing everyone off in one day as I tied my wet hair up in a ponytail and walked back to the dining room.

When I arrived, there were two place settings, but Adrienne was nowhere in sight. I decided to go into the kitchen to see if Iris needed any help. Big mistake. I found myself on the flat end of a very large, very hard wooden spoon as she chased me out. Apparently, while meals were being prepared, that area was her domain. I went back into the dining room to find Adrienne just sitting down.

I decided to try and make amends even though I still didn't know what to think of her ability to know things. I knew that I should have at least shown more respect. I looked at her with pleading eyes. "Adrienne, I was an ass today. Please, forgive me?"

"It's okay, Hayden. You don't need to apologize. It's not like I haven't gotten that kind of response before. I knew you would find out sooner or later, and I guess sooner was better than later."

It wasn't so much her words as it was the sadness behind them that made me feel like crap. I knew that I had deeply hurt her feelings. I suppose she had assumed I would be more understanding and supportive. In addition, I had washed a kitten and I thought I might never see him again. I was screwing up everything and was beginning to think I should set up residence somewhere more remote.

"Adrienne, I am truly sorry. I didn't understand. And to some degree I still don't, but I certainly can't look down on you for it. I don't want this to come between us. I don't know a lot about you, but I've enjoyed your company." I got down on my knees, trying to lighten the mood by giving her my best puppy-dog smile. "Please forgive me?"

"Get up off yo knees, chile," Iris barked as she entered the room. She grinned as she set two plates of food on the table.

"Iris, you don't have to wait on me, you know. I'm perfectly capable of fixing my own plate. Why don't you let me fix you a plate and then you can join us." I stood to make good on my offer.

She let out a good belly laugh, announced that "Iris don't be eatin' her own cookin', chile," then disappeared back into the domain, still laughing. That worried me. I looked at Adrienne, who couldn't hold back her reassuring smile.

"Don't worry, there's nothing wrong with her food. In fact, Iris is one of the best cooks on the island. She just doesn't like to eat what she cooks." Adrienne relieved my fears by taking a big bite of her dinner.

"So, are we okay now?" I asked, hoping for the best.

"I forgive you, Hayden, and yes, all is fine between us." She looked me in the eyes, smiled, and promptly changed the subject. "Is Calvin's new baby cute?"

I had to laugh. "Yes, as a matter of fact he is, but he has a big ol' box head like his daddy. Wow, it must have been a painful delivery for his mother. I assume everyone Calvin runs into has to look at the all those pictures of his wife and children?"

Her eyes twinkled as she smiled. "Yes, he doesn't miss an opportunity to show them off. He's a very proud papa."

"Adrienne, do you ever see yourself settling down with someone like Calvin and having kids? You obviously love them. I saw that yesterday when you took those little boys to the beach."

She sipped her wine before answering. "I do love children, and one day I hope to have some of my own. But I have no desire to be married to someone like Calvin. Although he is a very sweet man, and from what I can see, a loving husband and father."

"Then what's wrong with a man like him?" In my mind I silently begged for her to tell me what I wanted to hear.

"There's nothing wrong with Calvin. He's simply not my type," she responded with a coy expression.

I simply had to know, needed to hear the words. It was driving me crazy, so I took the plunge. "And just what exactly is your type?"

She laughed, and I could feel the blood drain to my feet. "I'm more interested in pursuing a relationship with a woman. Men do not interest me in the least."

There—she had said it, and now I knew we were on the same team. My knees started to bang together under the table, and my palms got sweaty. I had wanted to hear those words so badly, but having heard them, I was terrified. All the while I told myself to get over it; she probably wasn't interested in me anyway.

I swallowed nervously. "Oh. Well, I think that's great. I imagine the dating scene is a little skimpy in these parts, though."

She seemed to enjoy my awkwardness. "Is that your way of asking me if I'm taken?"

How could I come back on this one? My mind went blank, and to add to my uncomfortable predicament, her expression confirmed that she knew exactly what she was doing to me.

"I was just curious. You know, making conversation," I stammered. I had tried to sound casual, but failing miserably, all I could do was stare out at a palm tree and wish I was sitting in the top of it.

She smiled. "I see. Well, I have an advantage over you. As I'm sure you know, your aunt already told me of your preference for women. She also told me some very enlightening stories about some of your..." She paused for effect. "I suppose we could call them antics."

"Antics? What on earth did she tell you?" I dreaded the answer because my aunt was privy to some of my more naughty deeds.

"Well, for starters, she told me that she came to visit for the holidays one year when you were in high school."

I blushed at the vague memory of that night. My aunt had ushered me to my room and helped me get into bed. I threw up on her slippers. "I was just a teenager then. You can't hold that against me," I said smugly.

Her smile said she wasn't finished. "She also told me that your parents threw you out of the house because they came home unexpectedly and found something resembling an orgy in their living room."

"Hey! I can explain that! I was dating a college girl, and she had some sorority sisters that liked to—Never mind, I really can't explain that one away." I sighed. When I was young, sometimes I was just plain naughty.

I blushed and had to look away. "I was young and stupid then."

She giggled. "And now?"

"Well, now I'm older and stupid, but a lot tamer." I grinned.

"We should go to bed."

My jaw dropped open and nearly bounced off the table. I stared at her in total shock, replaying her words in my mind.

She realized how it must have sounded and her face turned blood red.

"Oh! I mean we have a busy day tomorrow. The guests will be coming the day after, and we need to make some final touches." Her face remained red even after she explained herself. She was adorable, and I knew from that moment on that I definitely had a thing for my business partner.

As we walked along the cobblestone pathway to our cottages, I was content to keep the conversation casual. I offered to walk her to her door since my cottage was the first on the path. She declined my offer and simply bade me good night. I couldn't resist peeking over my shoulder to watch her as she walked off.

I was met at the door by a very clean-smelling orange tabby. He had forgiven me, or at least his stomach had. There was a new gift too—a poor frog missing a leg and an eye. Saber's gift assured me that he had forgiven me for bathing him. He waited patiently as I got ready for bed. He cuddled up next to me and immediately drifted off to sleep. The sounds of his contented purr, despite his frog breath, lulled me to sleep.

The next morning I managed to sleep in until eight, when I was awakened by what sounded like heavy construction. I put on my robe, fed Saber, and went outside to see what the ruckus was about. There were people all over the place. Adrienne, radiant as ever, was standing in the middle of the courtyard talking to a man who had been power washing the courtyard and all the furniture.

Eager to join her, I showered and dressed, then took my coffee and went straight to the dining room where Iris informed me that I had missed breakfast and offered to cook me something. Not wanting to trouble her, I declined, opting for Count Chocula instead.

Iris sat at the table and read the paper. I had never studied her this closely. She was always in a flurry of movement, but as she sat there across from me, I was able to look her over. Her clothes were always neatly pressed, and most of her attire had a colorful tropical theme. I admired the long black hair that hung midway down her back. She was a heavy woman, with soft features and beautiful black skin that made the whites of her eyes stand out in stark contrast. Without saying a word, she radiated something that let you know she was a genuine and sincere person.

She glanced up from her paper and looked at me for a moment. "You gonna be hungry within da hour eatin' dat junk food, chile. You shoulda let Iris cook you some real food." She pulled a banana from the fruit bowl and slid it over to me while looking back at her paper. "Eat dat up 'fore you get up from dis table."

As I peeled the fruit, I gazed back at her. "Iris, what did you think of my aunt?"

She looked into my eyes and smiled. "I love dat woman. She is my best friend." She paused and stared off into space. I thought it strange that she had not referred to Gloria in the past tense.

"You mean she was your best friend?"

"No, chile. She *is* my best friend. She is here wit us. I can feel her all 'round. This place was and still is her home. At least dat is what I believe." She patted me on the shoulder and returned to the kitchen. Like Adrienne, when Iris was finished speaking, she simply walked away. And she wasn't concerned in the least whether you decided to mull over the conversation alone or think she was rude. Finished meant finished and nothing more.

After breakfast I went into the bar hoping to find Adrienne. Instead, I found a young woman mopping the bar. She explained to me that Adrienne was gathering flowers near our cottages. I met Adrienne on the pathway. She carried a huge basket of fresh-cut flowers and invited me along to help her put them in the guest cottages.

After we delivered the flowers, we filled the vases in the bar. The atmosphere around the inn was charged with excitement as each member of the staff came back on duty and added their own personal touches. The dining room and bar were festooned with decorations unique to the Bahamian culture.

Adrienne introduced me to the two porters and the cleaning and wait staff. Sarah, one of the cleaning ladies, took particular interest in the shirt I was wearing and complimented me on it. After asking if it would be all right if she touched the material, she gave it a little tug, her eyes like a child's as she studied the cloth.

It was a simple button-down shirt of lightweight stretchy cotton. The shade of yellow reminded me of springtime, which is what had prompted me to buy it. As I watched Sarah staring at it, I was reminded of how primitive this island actually was. There were no malls or outlet shops here, nor were there any banks or ATMs. I suppose that was why she took such an interest in it; it was just different.

Iris put on a big spread for lunch, and the entire staff joined us in the feast. The good-natured bantering around the table reminded me of a large family gathering. I remained quiet, listening to the stories and playful jibes. It took me a little while to understand what everyone was saying because of the Bahamian accent and the speed with which they talked.

I chuckled to myself. If my mom and dad had walked into the room that moment, they would have fainted dead away from shock. Adrienne and I were surrounded by people whose skin color contrasted sharply with our own. It simply didn't matter to any of us, but my dad would not have been pleased one whit. Well, that was his problem, as Aunt Gloria would have said. This was my new home and family, I was happy to be among them, and they seemed genuinely happy to have me. That's just how I liked it. I realized during that meal that I had more of Gloria in me than I did of my own parents.

To my dad, status in the community and image were the most important aspects of life, next to of course God. Gloria never cared about the trivialities, as she called her brother's obsession with appearances. Yet, in the eyes of these islanders, she had been nothing short of a saint. Her simple compassion had made an impact on nearly everyone who called this place home. I silently prayed that there was enough of my aunt in me to carry on her legacy.

After lunch we all went our separate ways to relax and mentally prepare for the arrival of the guests the following day. My only chore for the day was laundry. I stripped the bed and took my linens and clothes to the other side of the property, where I found the cottage that housed washers and dryers and an ice machine. Since none of the washers were in use, I took full advantage. I sorted my clothes into three separate piles and loaded up the washers.

I sat just outside the door and read for a while until the washers stopped. After everything was tumbling in the dryers, I settled down to read again. This was a great way to do the laundry, I mused. An hour later I finished folding the last of my things, and I had even pressed the yellow shirt I had worn earlier that day.

After I put the clothes away and made the bed, I felt ready to face the world. I was getting very used to this way of life. I grabbed the yellow shirt and went off on a mission. I found Sarah tending the plants in the courtyard.

"Hi, Sarah," I said as I walked up. She smiled and returned the greeting, her eyes darting to the shirt I was carrying. "I washed and pressed this today, and I would be honored if you would accept it as a gift. You seemed to like it earlier."

Her big brown eyes widened in surprise. "Oh, Hayden, I can't take your shirt. It's too pretty."

"Please, Sarah, I insist. Like I said, it's a gift."

"I can only accept it if you would be willing to make a trade." She smiled coyly as she unclasped the necklace that hung around her neck. It was beautiful in its simplicity: a bluish-purplish shell hanging from a simple silver chain. "Would you please consider accepting this as a trade for the shirt?"

"Sarah, does this necklace represent something special to you? If it does, the shirt is hardly worth it."

"No, not at all," she assured me. "I made it myself. I make all kinds of jewelry, and Adrienne is kind enough to allow me to put it in a display case for the guests to see."

"Well, in that case you have a deal." She helped me put the necklace on, and I was thrilled to have it. I gave her the shirt, and she hugged it close to her body. Then she gave me a quick hug and a kiss on the cheek. It made me feel good that the shirt made her so happy.

"Commits random acts of kindness" got added to my list. I needed some serious time alone to ponder my sanity; the bluff and the section of beach below it were perfect. Once I had skidded down the bluff, I tossed my sandals and kicked my feet through the cool sand along the edge of the surf. The beauty of the water never stopped amazing me.

I had been at this place for only a few days, and I hardly recognized myself. I wondered what was happening to me, but with the peacefulness I felt inside, I decided it couldn't be all that bad. I also questioned my feelings for Adrienne. She was a beautiful woman, but there was something else about her that drew me.

I had told myself how stupid it would be to get involved with someone I worked with. My mind acknowledged what my actions betrayed. When I was not in her presence, I realized how much I flirted with her. I should have never initiated the conversation last night at dinner. It made me appear interested, and if the truth be known, I was. More often than not, I found myself thinking about her. When I awoke each morning, my first thoughts were of her. When I fell asleep, the last thing I saw was her face. I tried to get my mind off her by burying my nose in a book, but it still managed to wander back right back to the auburn-haired beauty. I could have kicked myself for following after her like a schoolgirl. I was in the middle of a war: my sensibilities were battling with mind and emotions, not to mention my body.

Satisfied that I was completely alone, I confessed aloud that what was plaguing me was simply a juvenile crush and I needed to let it go. Even after hearing it pass my lips, I was still not completely convinced. *It would really help if she would stop looking at me the way she does.* Sometimes I swore she could see into my soul, and I was afraid I wouldn't measure up to her scrutiny.

When my stomach alerted me that dinner would be served soon, I turned and made my way back along the water's edge. Paradise, I was living in paradise, yet I was beginning to feel alone without Adrienne by my side. I hoped that the arrival of the guests would keep my mind occupied and that in a few days these feelings would pass. I crossed my fingers as I climbed the bluff to the inn, knowing that it wouldn't make any difference. I was hooked.

CHAPTER FOUR

The following morning Saber watched as I got dressed. I picked up the bedside clock from the floor, where he had slapped it the night before. Grumbling at the unique way of letting me know he wanted out, I made sure he had plenty of fresh water before I was off to greet the day. On my way to the dining room, I got caught up in the excitement of the impending arrival of our guests. I simply could not resist. I ran across the courtyard yelling at the top of my lungs. "Boss! De plane, de plane!"

Morning flew by, and around noon I met Adrienne in the bar. At any minute, the guests would be arriving, and I was more nervous about greeting them than I was going to admit. Adrienne seemed to sense my feelings and tried to reassure me.

In midsentence, she stopped talking. A peculiar expression crossed her face, but it was quickly replaced by a broad smile that lit up her eyes. She looked at me directly with such intensity that it made me squirm and fidget.

"You won't like one of the guests, but you have nothing to worry about," she said, with the grin still plastered across her face.

"Why would you say that? I haven't even met them yet. Oh wait; are you doing that thingy again?"

Before she could respond, the van pulled up in front of the bar. I felt just like Tattoo standing next to Mr. Roarke waiting for the guests. One of the porters opened the passenger doors and assisted the ladies as they got out. The other busied himself with their luggage, loading it on a golf cart to be taken to their cottages.

A tall, spiky-haired blonde, who resembled a Norwegian wrestler, rushed over and clamped Adrienne in a bear hug. Another woman nearly her size muscled in, peeled the blonde away, and vise-gripped Adrienne. She was tall but significantly less muscled than the wrestler. She had warm green eyes and a head full of long brown curly hair. Adrienne laughed and hugged them both, clearly enjoying the attention and warm greetings.

"Shelby, I'd like you to meet Hayden Tate, Gloria's niece."

When the tall blonde gave me my own personal bear hug, I swore she intended to break my ribs. She finally let me go and introduced me to Myra, her partner, who was significantly gentler in her embrace. My ribs were grateful.

The only word to describe the arrival of the guests was *pandemonium*. There were women everywhere, each taking turns hugging Adrienne like a long-lost relative. I actually felt sorry for her because just the few hugs I got left me breathless and sore. She was as gracious as ever and impressed our guests, and me as well, by remembering everyone's favorite drink.

We all piled into the bar, where Adrienne and I busted our butts filling drink orders. I had never tended bar before, though I had spent many hours on the opposite side. Needless to say, the view was quite different. I knew how to mix many of the drinks, but when someone ordered something exotic, all they got was rum and Coke. I did make the effort of throwing a little paper umbrella in each one. Of course they picked on me about this endlessly, but it was fun nevertheless.

Adrienne was right; there was one woman in particular I did not like. She stared—no, wait, *leered* at Adrienne from the minute she climbed out of the van. Adrienne didn't seem to notice the way the dark-eyed woman watched her every move.

It did not, however, escape me, and I fought the jealous feelings that rose up within.

I immediately began to pick her apart in my mind. I didn't like the way her beady brown eyes darted appraisingly over Adrienne. I didn't care for her style of dress either, which I deemed trashy. She was trying to hard to have everyone notice the breasts spilling out of her blouse which were more than likely man-made. I could have gone on for hours, but Adrienne interrupted my evaluation with another introduction.

Lunch was served in the bar, to the delight of everyone. Iris as always put on a beautiful spread of barbecued chicken and ribs with all the trimmings. I was delighted to note that there was no conch, but I knew somewhere along the line she would sneak it onto the menu.

There was so much chatter amongst the group that it was hard to carry on a conversation with the person next to me. The gang was silenced when Blair, a petite redhead, stood up on her chair and called for our attention. "Hayden, I just wanted to tell you on behalf of all of us that we were deeply saddened by the passing of your Aunt Gloria. We all loved her dearly, and her presence is sorely missed. Gloria always told us that you were a younger version of herself, and I have no doubt we will love you just as much as we did her."

The entire room erupted in applause. I felt my face turn bright red as everyone focused their attention on me. I stood and thanked them all for the sentiment, and then quickly sank low in my seat. Adrienne gave me a reassuring smile, but I knew it would be a while before my face returned to its normal color.

I could not help but notice that Dana, the woman who had been staring at Adrienne, had parked herself right next to her at lunch. I felt my blood boil as I noticed her stealing glances at Adrienne's cleavage. Though I had no right to be jealous, I still couldn't help it.

"I would like to propose a toast." A petite blonde sporting a red baseball cap stood and raised her glass. She was adorable, and I enjoyed the glimpse of her midriff as she stood there holding her glass in the air. "I raise my glass to our wonderful hostesses, my closest friends, and to the love of my life. May we continue this tradition of coming to Cat Island until we're too old to make it here." Everyone raised their glasses and cheered Rory for making such a toast.

A woman seated on the other side of me asked, "So, Hayden, what do you think of life here on the island? Have you fallen completely in love with it yet?" Katie. I remembered she was Dana's roommate. Immediately, I decided I didn't like her just by association.

Her looks annoyed me as well. She was also sporting a pair of silicone boobies and obviously took great pains to ensure them the freedom to roam loose out of her shirt. I like makeup, but I don't think it should be applied with a putty knife, which is exactly what she looked like she'd done. The eye makeup took the cake, though; she reminded me of a raccoon in heat.

"I'm beginning to get used to it. It's a far cry from home, though." I flashed my best fake smile as I answered.

"Well, you couldn't ask for a lovelier person to keep you company, could you?" Lacey responded.

The attention of the entire table had shifted to me, and I could feel my face turning red again.

"I have to agree with you there, Lacey. Iris has spoiled me rotten." I shot Adrienne a smirk. The table again erupted with laughter as Adrienne gave me a nod and a grin.

"Are we going to Nassau again this year?" Roslyn, also seated next to Adrienne, asked. "I'd love to do some more shopping in the open-air market near the port."

I was having a major problem matching all the names to the faces. I tried to pick a physical characteristic of each woman that would help me remember her name. Roslyn was very dark-complexioned and looked Hispanic. She had beautiful dark eyes and long dark hair. Neither she nor any of the other women had any excess body fat; they were all well toned, making me feel a little self-conscious.

Her stylishly dressed lover, Lacey, was absolutely beautiful. Had she been taller, I would have suspected she was a model. I liked her hair too. It was the same shade as mine, but straight, and hung just past her shoulders.

"Whoever wants to go, just sign up. I'll charter Bill Sampson's plane again," Adrienne answered to shouts of glee and a few moans from the nonshoppers.

I was tickled pink. I knew that Nassau had a Pizza Hut, and my heart skipped double time at the thought of a gooey deep-dish pizza. I dearly loved Iris's cooking, but a girl has to have her pizza fix.

After lunch, the group broke up and everyone went to unpack. Adrienne and I helped the wait staff clean up the bar, then relaxed on the chaise lounges and took a break.

"Were you able to commit any of their names to memory?" she teased.

"I remember the first two I was introduced to. Especially Shelby because of the rib-breaking bear hug she gave me. After that, it all became a blur. I did, however, remember one other name. Dana, the dark-haired woman sitting next to you at lunch."

"Oh? Did she spark your interest? You do realize she is one of two single women in the group."

"I can assure you that she does not interest me in the least, but she does seem very interested in a certain green-eyed beauty that we both know. I think she went to great lengths to prove that already."

Adrienne flashed a big, toothy grin. "Why does she get under your skin so?"

She was baiting me to admit I was jealous, and I had no intention of losing the game. Although I did find it intriguing that she wanted me to come clean. "I don't like women who make it obvious they're on the prowl." I thought I might have gained a point on that one and fought the urge to grin.

"Maybe she's not prowling. Perhaps she's looking for something substantial and is simply trying to be noticed." She flashed that grin at me again. Little wiseass. I was a bigger ass than she, and I aimed to prove it.

"Unless I'm blind, she has you in her sights. She's only here for two weeks, so that suggests to me that all she's looking for is a little tropical fling." I felt especially triumphant with that answer.

"A lot of feelings can develop in a short period of time, Hayden. Maybe she knows if she plays her cards right, she won't be leaving this island a single woman." She stood and looked down at me, no longer grinning. "I have some things to do before we have to prepare for dinner. I'll see you a little later."

I sat there a long time chain-smoking. Adrienne had played the game well and had emerged the victor. Her words rocked me to the core. Would she really consider leaving Cat Island? I was naïve to think that she would want to remain single forever. If she left, I wondered if this place would have the same appeal. I was beginning to understand what she meant by feelings that developed in a short time.

I climbed behind the bar and played bartender when a few of the girls wandered back into the bar for another drink. They sat around chatting and before I knew it, I was drawn into the conversation.

It amazed me what a bartender learned while on the job. I was surprised to discover how loose-lipped people got when they had a few drinks under their belts. I wondered how much I had babbled off when I had bellied up to the bars I used to frequent.

I was especially happy to hear that these girls were growing disenchanted with Dana, and I listened with great interest. Leigh was aggravated by the way Dana had flirted with her lover during their flight to the island. I tried to remember which one her partner was as I pretended to be uninterested in the subject.

If I had been Dana, I would have thought twice about crossing Leigh, who was only about five feet tall but had the arms and legs of someone who worked out nonstop. With her hair back in a ponytail and those muscles, she was ready for a kickboxing ring at any minute.

"Did you notice the way Dana pawed at Blair nearly the entire flight here? I have no problem with them having a chat, but the way Dana touched her every time she said something was really beginning to piss me off." Leigh scowled.

Leigh reminded me that her partner was the redhead who had made the little speech about my aunt when they arrived. I remembered Blair then because she had the cutest spattering of freckles across her nose. I committed that couple to memory. Lacey and Roslyn were also at the bar, and they made their couple status quite obvious by pawing at each other. I pretended to be only mildly interested in their conversation, but as Leigh continued, I felt the hair on the back of my neck rise up. I had just met Dana, but my reaction was instant: an almost uncontrollable urge to kick her ass up between her shoulders. She had shown definite interest in Adrienne and made it blatantly obvious to anyone who had eyes. I quickly made up my mind that I was not about to compete against this rubber-breasted bitch, and a good old fashioned ass whipping was in her immediate future if she didn't back off.

Roslyn and Lacey told Leigh that they had noticed it as well and that some of the other girls had made mention of it too. Then came the kicker—it came to light why Dana was on Cat Island without a mate: her former lover had caught her in bed with another woman. The conversation that followed only confirmed what I already knew. Dana was a ho!

Bored with trashing the black sheep of the group, they turned their attention to me. "So, are you and Adrienne an item yet?" Lacey asked with a shrewd smile as a frisky Roslyn nibbled on her earlobe.

I tried not to blush. "I've only been here a week. We hardly know one another yet," I said as I nervously wiped the bar.

Roslyn was quick to pipe up, and I suspected that the women intended to play matchmaker. "She was keeping a close eye on you at lunch today. I'm not completely convinced that you two aren't hiding something. You had better keep her close; Dana has already made some choice comments about the lovely Miss Adrienne."

I barely kept a low, guttural growl from escaping my throat. I was spared from having to respond by Adrienne's perfectly timed arrival. "I see you girls are being well taken care of," she said cheerfully as she walked into the bar.

Roslyn winked at me. "Hayden has been doing a wonderful job as bartender. Fortunately for us, we're all drinking rum and Coke." I debated popping her with a bar towel.

"Sit down and talk with us, Adrienne." Leigh pulled out a bar stool.

Roslyn wore a devilish grin as she turned her attention to Adrienne. "So. Ahem. Tell us about you and the bartender. Don't lie and say there's nothing going on between you two. We watched you both at lunch, and neither of you seemed able to keep your eyes off each other."

That did it. I grabbed a glass and filled it nearly to the top with bourbon and added a dash of Coke. I watched as Adrienne's face started to match the reds in the bird of paradise plant just behind her. She nervously tucked her hair behind her ears.

"I was just keeping an eye on Hayden, that's all. The inn business is all new to her, and she's just getting her feet wet. Right, Hayden?" She looked at me for confirmation, but before I could speak Leigh joined the attack.

"Adrienne, darling, your eyes were glued to her ass until she sat down," she said with a wicked grin. I laughed right along with them even though my heart was beating out of my chest.

When Adrienne regained the ability to speak she narrowed her eyes at Leigh. "I was most certainly not staring at her ass!" She tried to maintain her serious expression, but finally a sheepish grin made its way across her features.

"You're both terrible liars. You can cut the sexual tension between you two with a knife. If you haven't taken a roll in the hay, you're not far from it. Now tell us the truth." Roslyn looked at me for an explanation.

I stood there with my jaw clicking for a moment, then took a big swallow of my drink. I grabbed a cigarette and winced when I realized they were all waiting for me to speak, including Adrienne.

"Um...I...uh...We really haven't discussed anything like that," I stammered as I plotted a way to escape with what was left of my dignity.

"Don't you think it's time you two start discussing things? Gloria used to tell me all the time that you both would hit it off. You've been here alone together for almost a week, and I refuse to believe that you two have been totally innocent." Leigh gave Adrienne a playful nudge.

"We have been innocent. We've been too busy getting ready for your arrival to do anything else." Adrienne's neck had begun to flush. I wasn't sure if she was embarrassed or downright pissed off.

"Well then, allow us to help you both out." Roslyn waved off Adrienne's attempts to shut her up. "Hayden, do you find her attractive?"

"Um, well, of course I do. I mean, who wouldn't? Just look at her." I couldn't even look at Adrienne. I actually debated setting the wicker siding on fire just to have an excuse to run.

"All right. Now, Adrienne." Roslyn grinned as Adrienne nervously twisted her hair again. "I think it's pretty obvious you find Hayden attractive. I imagine there are some very impure thoughts going on in that pretty little head of yours."

Adrienne jumped up from her bar stool, nearly knocking it over. "We'll have to finish this conversation later. I have to go tend to some things." She turned and walked out of the bar, ignoring the taunts from Roslyn and Leigh.

"I think we may have pushed green eyes a little too far with that one," Leigh said with a laugh. She turned and gave me a look that said I was not out of the woods yet.

"Hayden, she likes you. You need to let her know you're interested. On the ride in from the airstrip, Dana explained in great detail what she wanted to do to her if she got her alone for a second. None of us wants to see that happen—not that Adrienne would be interested anyway, but you still need to talk to her."

"Leigh, I don't want to mess things up with her by moving too fast. Besides, you may say she's interested, but I don't know that for sure."

"We've been coming here for years. Single women have accompanied us before, but Adrienne never looked at them the way she does you. She's very interested, so stop beating around the bush and get busy," Roslyn said as Leigh nodded vigorously.

I had not realized how much time had passed while I was bartending. Adrienne informed us that dinner would be served in thirty minutes. We all went our separate ways to get cleaned up. I decided it wouldn't be a bad idea to take a quick shower and change my clothes. I made it back to the dining room a little late to find it nearly full. Adrienne had kindly saved me a seat, although I felt my hackles rise when I saw Dana perched on the other side of her. For some reason, I was reminded of a starving buzzard hovering over road kill.

Dinner was much like lunch. The crowd was so boisterous that it was hard to follow any one conversation. That was especially irritating because I had to strain to hear what Dana was saying to Adrienne, who politely listened to the buzzard drone on about her career as a legal secretary. I hoped that Adrienne was as unimpressed as I was.

We were all sitting pretty close, and occasionally Adrienne's leg would brush against mine. I noticed that she had scooted her chair a little closer to mine, but I told myself that it was only because she didn't want to be that close to Dana.

After dinner, we all went into the bar where Sarah had already set up to pour drinks. Music played on the sound system that I didn't know we had. The group decided that calypso music was not what they had in mind, and someone produced a CD with dance music. Before long, our cozy little bar had been transformed into a disco.

Not being one to dance, I volunteered to assist Sarah. I stuck with the easy drinks and left the more complex requests up to her. I kept an eye on the ho as she continued to try and impress Adrienne. I growled in disgust at that stupid smile she kept flashing.

"I think Adrienne has an admirer," Sarah said when she caught me staring at them.

"It sure looks that way, doesn't it?" I tried to hide the resentment in my voice.

"I wouldn't worry about that woman. She's not the one for Adrienne. Her heart already has been won by another." Sarah winked as she filled another drink order. I wanted to drop everything and make Sarah elaborate, but I had my hands full making rum and Cokes.

Shelby managed to coax Adrienne out onto the makeshift dance floor and sandwiched her between herself and Myra. I couldn't help but stare as they moved seductively. I also noticed that Dana was watching with interest. I could see the lust in her eyes and wondered if my own revealed the same.

I tried not to make it obvious that I was watching Adrienne, but I found it hard not to look at her body pressed so tightly against Myra's backside. Adrienne's hands rested on Myra's hips; Shelby was behind Adrienne and was pressed against her just as snugly. They moved in time with the music, and I found it impossible to tear my eyes from them. Adrienne turned, her eyes met mine, and I was powerless to look away. We held each other's gaze as the three women moved sensuously to the music.

My skin flushed, and I could feel little beads of sweat break out on my upper lip. Adrienne was already sweaty from dancing, and her bangs hung in wet tendrils across her forehead. Seeing her like that conjured up all sorts of sexual images in my mind, and my eyes stayed locked with hers until I was interrupted by someone at the bar.

Donna, a cute blonde with pretty blue eyes that I remembered as being Chelsey's girlfriend, was taking a break from the floor and resting at the bar. She was a paramedic, so I committed her to memory by picturing her wearing only a uniform shirt and stethoscope. That image, alluring as it was, still did little to keep my thoughts from the auburn-haired beauty on the dance floor.

"So, Hayden, will you be participating in the first-night tradition with us?" Donna asked.

I was a little confused as to what she was talking about since Adrienne had made no mention of any kind of tradition. "I don't know. I guess it depends on the tradition," I responded, hoping she would fill me in. My eyes drifted back to the floor as the music changed to a more upbeat song.

My heart nearly stopped when the little blonde laughed and said, "At midnight, we all go down to the beach and skinny-dip. I can't believe Adrienne didn't tell you."

The thought of seeing Adrienne naked and bathed in moonlight was very appealing. "I don't do naked." I laughed. "You could not get me drunk enough to get me naked in front of all of you." Still, it was tempting.

Then Donna did the unthinkable. She reached over and cut the music off, causing everyone to turn and look. Then she yelled, "Hayden is too shy to go skinny-dipping with us. I suggest we get her drunk and make her join the crowd."

The group as a whole rushed the bar and pulled me out from behind it. Someone turned the music back on, and before I knew it I had a drink in my hand. Each couple adopted me as their pet for a while and made sure I had plenty to drink. By midnight I was as drunk as a skunk.

I had stuck another cigarette between my lips, but before I could light it someone reached over and plucked it out of my mouth. I turned to see who the thief was and met a pair of striking green eyes.

"I know you don't like to dance, but this is a slow song." Adrienne took my hand and pulled me close to her. "Even you can slow dance, Hayden," she said as she pulled my hands up to rest behind her neck. I could feel her breath on my face and caught a hint of alcohol. Her tight grip around my waist and the way her body moved against mine told me that she was every bit as lit as I was. I couldn't imagine a sober Adrienne behaving that way.

There was very little breeze that night, and the least bit of exercise caused us all to sweat—although I doubted the temperature had very much to do with the way my body heated up next to Adrienne. I rested my hands behind her shoulders, and I could feel the dampness of her shirt against my hands. I was a little shorter than she, so my forehead rested against her cheek. The thought of being like this with her horizontally made me unconsciously clutch her shirt.

She pulled back a little and looked me in the eyes questioningly. I couldn't say a word, just stared back. Another couple brushed against us, shifting me a little to the side. Adrienne's leg moved between mine as she continued to press her body snugly into mine, causing me to groan.

My gaze slowly descended from her eyes to her lips, which were parted slightly and looked oh so inviting. She slid her hand farther up my back and pressed me closer into her until our lips were only inches apart. When the desire to kiss her for the first time overwhelmed me, I leaned in slowly until I felt the lightest brush of softness. Suddenly, I felt a hand grab the back of my shirt and I was torn from her arms.

In my drunken stupor, I realized I was being herded toward the beach by a rowdy bunch of drunken lesbians. Not far ahead of me I could see Adrienne being hauled along by Shelby and a few others. I was in trouble, big-time. I was about to be made to get naked in front of a group of total strangers. Not to mention the fact that Adrienne would be there.

My protests fell on deaf ears as the wild bunch half dragged me through the sand, chanting some rap song that had played in the bar. I felt like I was being led to some driftwood altar where I was going to be offered up in a pagan sacrifice to the conch-shell god.

Clothes flew as the women all began to strip. There was no escape for me as a small herd of them gathered around me and pulled at my clothes. I looked around for Adrienne and was happy to see she was suffering the same fate. Once they had stripped me, I shot off like a rocket to the water to hide my white butt, which lit up the beach like a Q-Beam. A dozen leaping lesbians jumped and played in the water. I had been dunked twice already and felt up once before I got the bright idea to swim out a little.

The coolness of the water had sobered me up considerably, and I was standing on my toes trying to stay far enough back from the rambunctious games when a familiar voice whispered in my ear. "Protect me from Dana; she wants to get to know me better." I turned to see Adrienne trying to hide her lanky body behind mine.

"Are they always like this?" I asked in surprise.

Adrienne laughed. "Yes, every year it's the same thing, and I'm sure you know now they don't take no for an answer."

"Does that include Dana?"

"Especially Dana. That's precisely why I'm hiding behind you."

"Is that the only reason you came over to me?" I asked, regretting it as it came out of my mouth.

"No, it's—" Her voice dissolved into gurgling as Rory and Allison double-teamed her and dunked her under the water. As I realized what had happened, my feet were pulled out from under me and down I went. When I broke the surface, Rory and Allison were cackling with laughter as they sought their next victims.

I had lost my foothold and was struggling to tread water when a pair of arms wrapped around my waist. "Sucks to be short, doesn't it," Adrienne teased as she kept my head above water. I couldn't come back with a wisecrack, overwhelmed at how good it felt to have her naked body pressed against mine.

When I didn't readily respond, she said, "I don't think there's any hope of us escaping with our dignity tonight. Hopefully we'll fare better tomorrow night."

"Tomorrow night?"

"This is a ritual for them. They get drunk, and then they come to the beach and skinny-dip. No sense in hiding; they'll hunt you down and drag you out here every night."

All the blood in my body was rushing south, and it was increasingly difficult for me to form a coherent sentence. Adrienne made no move to release me, and her warm breath on my neck was causing all sorts of reactions. When I finally did relax and gave in to the sensation of her so close against me, the crowd had begun to tire and get out of the water.

The last of the gang left, but Adrienne still hadn't moved away. I wondered if she was holding me there because she was enjoying it as much as I was, or if she was simply hiding from Dana. My heart sank as I felt her arms slip away.

"I think it's safe for us to make a break for it now."

"You get out first," I said as I hung back, protecting my modesty.

"Okay, but don't look." She waded ashore and collected her clothes. The temptation to peek was nearly unbearable, but I managed to obey. Finally, she told me I could turn around, and then she looked away as I walked on shore and pulled my sandy clothes over my wet body. This took care of any exfoliating needs I might have had for a month.

We climbed the bluff in silence, and when we reached the top she finally spoke. "Hayden?" Her voice interrupted my reminiscing of the evening's events. "Were your panties missing too?"

I laughed out loud. "Yep, and my bra. Is this another one of their rituals?"

She laughed nervously. "No. My undergarments have never come up missing before. I'm afraid that we'll find them displayed somewhere around the inn tomorrow, or worse, someone took them for a keepsake."

We arrived at her cottage first, and I found myself getting nervous all over again. How would I end this evening? "Um, Adrienne?" I mumbled nervously. "Thank you for rescuing me earlier tonight."

She smiled as her eyes settled on mine. "It was all my pleasure, Hayden. I need to thank you as well for hiding me from Dana." At that very moment we heard it. The unmistakable cries of passion being carried to us on the wind from one or more of the guest cottages.

"Is that what I think it is?" I asked as my face colored.

"Yes." Her face turned red as well, and her eyes could no longer meet mine. We stood there in an awkward silence for a moment and then began to giggle like teenagers.

"Hayden, you know what's really bad about this?" She snorted. "Since we have no air-conditioning, we'll be hearing this most of the night."

We both fell into a fit of laughter as the chorus of unfettered moans and groans grew louder. Either the other women didn't hear us, or they just didn't care. When we regained our composure, awkwardness settled over us again.

"Well, good night, Adrienne," I said with regret, and started toward my cottage.

"Good night, Hayden, and thank you for a wonderful evening."

I can only describe my thoughts as a giant cluster fornication. My sensibilities waged war with my libido. I was tempted to turn and run back to her, but my mind fought against it. Finally, fear popped up and made me wonder if she would reject me. That was enough to send me straight to my cottage, where I spent a while in a cold shower.

I climbed into bed and was quickly joined by Saber—not my choice of bedmates that night, but I welcomed the company. I lay there for a long time trying to purge my mind of the thoughts that had plagued me all day. The most unsettling was the thought of Adrienne meeting someone and leaving the island. The most arousing was the memory of her body pressed against mine earlier that evening. That, coupled with the howler monkeys having sex two cottages over, made for a very sleepless night.

I woke up the following morning at nine and let Saber out. I was relieved that Iris and her staff were reliable and would to tend to the needs of our guests without our supervision, although I seriously doubted that any of the group would be getting up early.

I started the coffee and climbed back into bed and didn't move until Saber scratched at the door. He was ready for breakfast. Following my new morning routine, I sat on the doorstep and sipped my coffee and lit up a cigarette. I needed to acquire some lawn chairs, because sitting on the threshold every day was making a permanent indentation on my ass.

To my surprise and supreme delight, Adrienne came over seeking coffee, her coffeemaker having given up the ghost. We both sat out on the step, hoping the coffee would silence the steel-drum bands that were pounding away inside our skulls. As we sat there making small talk, Dana walked by, dressed like she was going for a morning walk or jog—but obviously headed for Adrienne's cottage.

I felt the hairs rise up on the back of my neck, but the look on her face when she saw both of us sitting there in our robes was priceless. I had to fight the urge to laugh in her face. She gave us a nod and kept walking.

Adrienne looked at me mischievously. "She thinks we slept together." Then she chuckled. "If you don't mind, I'd like her to think that's the truth. Maybe then she'll leave me alone."

"Only on one condition will I agree to that." Adrienne nodded in agreement. "You tell everybody I rolled your eyes up in your head so many times that you won't be able to see straight for weeks."

Adrienne burst into a fit of laughter. I shot her my best indignant look. "You laugh like you doubt my abilities!" I said in mock indignation.

"The proof is in the pudding, sweetie," she shot back, with that same mischievous glint in her eye.

"I've never employed pudding in my lovemaking. Do you roll around in it or just apply it?" I said as she stood to leave.

"You're such a smart-ass, Hayden, which is one of your more endearing qualities." She grinned. "Thank you for the coffee. I'm off to shower. Will I see you at breakfast?"

"Yep. I'll be there unless Iris is serving conch pancakes—then you can count me out. Will you save me a seat?"

"I always do." She smiled and then walked away. I watched the sexy sway of her hips and wondered what she had on under that robe.

As I showered, I remembered the look on Dana's face earlier, and laughed out loud, which set off a chain of events: I inhaled some of the lather that was on my face and began to choke, the soap found its way into my eyes, and then I fell out of the shower, landing square in the middle of the bathroom floor where Saber looked at me as though I pulled this stunt every morning. I guess my mom was right, you should never make fun of someone else's misfortune.

Even after the shower incident, I was in high spirits as I skipped across the courtyard on the way to breakfast. A damper closed on my good mood when I saw that Dana was sitting next to Adrienne at the table. The muscles in my face twitched as I tried to keep my expression neutral. This ho would not give up.

I made small talk with a couple of the girls, but my mind seethed with hostility toward Dana, who had her hand resting atop Adrienne's as she spoke. I did my best to calm myself by picturing Dana with two pieces of bacon shoved up her nostrils. Adrienne choked on her juice and had to excuse herself from the table, and I quickly followed her into the kitchen.

"Are you all right?"

Adrienne's face was beet red, and she appeared to be laughing between gasps for air. "Hayden, who's a buck-toothed, biscuit-eating bitch?" she asked as tears poured down her face.

"You really can hear my thoughts, can't you?"

She nodded as she continued to wipe her face and regain her composure. "It just came booming through my head," she said and began to laugh again.

"I heard someone say that once, and it's certainly befitting of the woman sitting next to you at the table. I don't like her. And no one else but Katie likes her either. Let's send her nasty ass home."

Adrienne blotted her eyes and took a sip of water. "We can't run off guests just because we don't like them, that's all part of running a business like this. It's only two weeks, and then she'll be gone. Try to make the best of it." She took my hand and led me back to the dining area.

CHAPTER FIVE

It occurred to me that I was getting fairly possessive of a woman without having any idea how she felt about me. The previous night had piqued my curiosity, and sitting next to Adrienne that morning while remembering that didn't help any either. I desperately sought something to take my mind off her and struck up a conversation with some of the girls.

I was amazed at the energy our guests possessed. All of them looked and acted as though they had a full night's rest. I knew for a fact that two of them hadn't because they'd kept me awake until the wee hours of the morning.

I was happy to hear that they were all leaving after breakfast. Some of them were going diving, and the rest were going shopping. I said my good-byes as the porters loaded them into the vans and took them on their merry way. Adrienne and I then went to help the staff clean up.

The guests had planned to eat lunch in town, so we didn't have to worry about entertaining them until later on in the day. Adrienne and I settled down for a break on a couple of chaise lounges in the bar, and soon, both of us drifted off into some much-needed sleep. I woke up a couple of hours later to find Adrienne still in dreamland. I watched her as she slumbered, wanting very badly to reach out and feel her soft skin.

As much as I loved the relaxed atmosphere of this place, I had to come to terms with the fact that the only thing keeping me from selling my half and leaving was the woman lying beside me. In less than a week's time, she had unknowingly wrapped me around her little finger. I tried to pass it off as simple lust, but in my heart, I knew it went much deeper than that.

She stirred and slowly opened her eyes. She caught me looking at her and smiled. I knew she had no earthly idea what she did to me when she looked at me like that. Neither of us said anything but simply stared at the other. I was afraid to utter a word for fear of breaking the spell.

"I have an idea. Why don't we pack a lunch and go down to the beach and be bums?" She rubbed her sleepy eyes.

"Sounds like a plan to me." I stood and offered to help her up, enjoying the feel of her hand in mine.

We both sneaked into the kitchen, knowing that if Iris caught us we'd get the wooden-spoon treatment. We threw together a couple of sandwiches, grabbed a big bag of chips and some drinks, and crept out into the bar with our loot. Once we were sure the coast was clear, we made a break for the courtyard. Halfway across, something hard hit the back of my thigh. I yelped in surprise and wheeled around.

"Stay outta my kitchen, girlies, or you'll get more than that next time," Iris said as she wagged her finger. I looked at the ground and next to my foot was the wooden spoon. Iris was nothing if not accurate.

Adrienne and I laughed like two little girls caught robbing the cookie jar and made a run for it. We stopped off at our cottages, changed into our swimsuits, and headed for the beach.

Adrienne decided to go a little farther down from where the staff had set up umbrellas and chairs and a volleyball net. We walked a fair distance down the beach until she found the spot she wanted. A little warm from our hike, we went straight for the water.

There was something incredibly serene about swimming alone with her. I had to fight the urge to stare at her while she swam gracefully on the surface. Except for the noise we made, there were only the sounds of the water and of nature itself. We spent a while relaxing in the surf and enjoying the peace of being alone until hunger drove us to the beach.

After we ate, we lay on the beach talking. We laughed at the antics of our guests and wondered what kind of mischief they would get into that night. The topic eventually turned to Dana, and I had to ask the question that had been on my mind since the guests arrived.

"Adrienne, did you know specifically that Dana would be the one I didn't like?"

"No, I had no idea which one it would be." Adrienne stared out at the water. "The thought occurred to me that there would be one that would make you jealous." She turned her eyes to me.

"Is that why you smiled like the cat that ate the canary when you told me that before they arrived?" I looked away, afraid to meet her gaze.

"Are you asking me if I liked that you were jealous of another woman's interest in me?"

I could see out of the corner of my eye that she was looking directly at me with a big grin spreading across her face. Unable to look back into her eyes, I stared straight ahead at the water.

"Yes, that is exactly what I want to know." I pretended to be interested in a shell that I randomly picked up.

"Then the answer is yes. I liked knowing that she made you jealous. At least it was some indication that you were vaguely interested in me."

Hearing her admission tied my stomach into knots. "Is it safe to assume you're interested in me too?" I asked.

She reached over and gently stroked my cheek, forcing me to look her in the eyes.

"I have a confession to make, Hayden. Your aunt spent hours talking about you. She read me all of your letters, showed me all the pictures you sent, and even told me the silly and sometimes dirty jokes you told her. I felt like I knew you before you ever got here. I've been interested in you for years."

I couldn't believe what I was hearing and stared at her incredulously. My heart nearly pounded out of my chest while I looked into her eyes and saw the sincerity.

"Your aunt left the inn to you because she knew you would carry on the traditions she started. But there was another reason. She told me that she knew in her heart we would be perfect for each other."

"Is it true, Adrienne?" I dug my fingers into the sand as I awaited her answer. It seemed as though my entire future hung on the words she would utter. Even so, I thought myself a fool feeling that way about someone I had only known a week.

"I know that it's true. I knew it before you got here. Remember, I have that thingy, as you so eloquently put it." She smirked. "I just know. I've been waiting for you to come to the same realization. Now I want to know, do you believe it's true?"

I felt like I was being sucked inside a whirlpool, and I had to shake my head to stop the spinning. Before I could reason or dissect my thoughts, I heard the words spill from my mouth. "Yes, Adrienne, I do believe it's true."

I sat there stunned for a few minutes. One side of me was elated because this woman stirred feelings within me that I'd never felt before. The other side of me was completely terrified. The tug-of-war left me as light-headed as the laughing gas I require at the dentist's office. The only thing missing now was the little pig-nose mask.

"Where do we go from here?" I asked, trying to make sense of it all. She smiled and nervously ran her fingers through her wet hair.

"There's no need to hurry. I think we should let things happen as we get more comfortable with the way we feel. Although at this moment, I want to know what it's like to kiss you."

Her face drew closer to mine. I closed my eyes when I felt the press of her soft lips—the feeling was so exquisite that my skin broke out in goose bumps. When her tongue slipped across my bottom lip, I had to fight to keep my body from trembling.

I had kissed many women, but none of those kisses compared to what I experienced on the beach that day. Then she pulled away from me and looked into my eyes and opened her mouth to speak. I was expecting to hear her say something romantic, but she surprised me when she said, "The gang is back."

I smiled. "Is that thingy at work again?"

"No, Dana's standing on the beach watching us."

This time I made no effort to stop the growl that rose up from my chest. I turned to glare at Dana, who thought better of approaching us and made her way back up the bluff. If my aunt were watching us, I knew she was rolling with laughter.

"Well, so much for rest and relaxation," Adrienne said as she gathered our things. She took my hand in hers and we strolled along the water's edge. Something as simple as holding her hand sent a rush of emotions through me that thrilled me to the core. I felt like a giddy teenager who was embarking on the adventure of first love.

We went to our own cottages and showered and dressed for dinner. As we walked to the bar, Adrienne took my hand in hers again. There was no mistaking that we were a couple, and the knowing glances we received when we arrived confirmed that. Dana didn't look too happy, and it took every ounce of the adult in me to not stop, shake my butt, and yell, "nah nah nah!"

There was a wonderful breeze blowing in off the water as Iris served dinner in the bar. Our usual seating arrangement had been forsaken for the night, and I found myself sitting between Rory and Allison. I felt a little sorry for Adrienne because Leigh and Roslyn had her surrounded, and from the flush on her face I could tell they were picking her apart again. I strained to hear the conversation that was making her face turn so many shades of red.

"Adrienne, you stop it now." Leigh grabbed both of Adrienne's hands, forcing her to look into her eyes. "We saw you on the dance floor last night. And in the water."

"You two were holding hands today too," Roslyn added.

"Just because we danced together and held hands doesn't mean we slept together, for Pete's sake," Adrienne said in exasperation.

"You can't sit there and look me in the eye and say you didn't get into her pants. If you two had danced a little longer last night you would have probably done her in the middle of the dance floor!" Leigh laughed.

Adrienne gasped. "Do you both think I'm some sort of sex maniac? That I can't control myself around someone I'm attracted to?"

"Okay, when was the last time you had sex?"

Adrienne laughed. "That's none of your business, Roslyn. This whole conversation is none of your business."

"Cut the shit, Adrienne. We've had some very intimate conversations over the years, and the fact that you're so evasive when we ask you about Hayden tells me something's going on. Now fess up. When was the last time you had sex?" Leigh pressed.

"Do you mean by myself or with someone else?"

Roslyn pinched Adrienne's arm. "With a real human being, and battery-operated devices do not count."

Adrienne sighed. "It's been so long I've forgotten what it feels like."

"Then what's keeping you from throwing Hayden down and getting busy? Are you waiting on a marriage proposal?"

"Well, what are you suggesting I do, Leigh? Do you want me to go and bend her over one of the tables right now?"

Roslyn and Leigh both laughed. Then Roslyn looked at Adrienne with an evil grin. "Not right now, but you might want to consider that later when you get back to your cottage."

All three of them turned and looked my way at the same time and caught me watching them. Adrienne gave me a quick smile and looked away. The other two exchanged glances and then looked back at me. I swallowed hard, knowing they planned to interrogate me next.

Once the dinner dishes were cleared away, we pushed the tables back and the middle of the bar turned into a dance floor once again. I started toward the bar to mix drinks and protect myself from the matchmakers, but before I could get there I felt a hand on my arm and was not surprised to see Leigh.

"Come sit down with me and have a drink, Hayden." I didn't like the looks of that grin she flashed and glanced around searching for Adrienne. Roslyn had already pulled her out onto the dance floor. I was trapped.

Leigh led me to a table and set a bottle of rum down in front of me. "Don't even use a glass, baby, this bottle is all yours."

Nervous, I took a big swallow from the bottle and sat there with teary eyes as the alcohol burned all the way down to my toes. With liquid courage racing through my veins, I looked Leigh in the eyes. "No, we haven't slept together," I blurted out.

The song ended, and Roslyn and Adrienne joined us. Roslyn pulled out the chair next to me and motioned for Adrienne to sit. Then she went over to the bar. Adrienne leaned over and whispered in my ear, "They're in rare form tonight. Heaven help us both."

Roslyn returned with a box of shot vials. "Who's up for body shots?"

The bar erupted in a roar. Roslyn gave us a grin. "You two pay attention and let a pro show you how it's done." She grabbed Lacey by the hand and planted her in a chair, then straddled her lap. Lacey unbuttoned Roslyn's shirt while the crowd around us cheered them on.

Roslyn slipped a vial down into her cleavage, anchoring it in her bra. Then she seductively slipped her shirt off. Lacey kissed her way down the front of her chest, and when she put her mouth on the vial, Roslyn leaned forward and poured the liquor down her throat. The crowd cheered as Lacey held the empty vial in her teeth. "Who's next?" she called out after putting the vial on the table.

"We'll do it." Chelsey had Donna take off her shirt and lie down on the table in front of us. "Give me a shot of tequila," Chelsey ordered as she positioned herself between Donna's legs. She took a lime and squeezed a liberal trail of juice down Donna's chest to her belly button.

"Baby! This is my favorite bra!" Donna complained.

"Then take it off," Chelsey taunted as she sucked lime juice off her fingers. The crowd chanted, "Take it off! Take it off!" To my surprise, she did.

As I sat there bug-eyed at the topless blonde laid out on the table, Leigh shoved the bottle of rum in my face and ordered me to drink. Roslyn was giving Adrienne the same treatment. My heart began to beat double time when I realized that they intended for Adrienne and me to do body shots as well. I would have loved to lick her from head to toe, that I couldn't deny, but not in front of an audience.

Chelsey poured the shot of tequila over Donna's breasts and down her stomach, where some of it pooled in her belly button. She lowered her head and drank the alcohol out of Donna's navel, then licked her way up to her breasts. My jaw nearly hit the floor when she licked each breast clean. If they kept up at this rate, we'd have a full-blown orgy going on by midnight.

"So, Adrienne, you ready to take a turn yet?" Roslyn asked with a gleam in her eye.

"Oh, hell no!" She tried to get up from her chair, but Roslyn gave her a little shove back down.

Leigh and Blair decided to go next. With a little goading from the group, Blair stripped off her shirt and bra and lay down across the table. She spread her legs as Leigh slid between them and squeezed a lime wedge, spilling the juice down her body as Chelsey had done to Donna. Then Leigh poured the tequila shot down Blair's body and sipped the drink from her navel. She took her time and slowly licked every drop from Blair's skin, spending a long time on her breasts. Then, to one-up Chelsey and Donna, she poured another shot into her mouth and let it spill from her lips into Blair's mouth.

The crowd cheered, and everyone wanted to know who was next. Adrienne and I both sank down into our chairs, hoping to go unnoticed. Leigh grabbed the front of my shirt and pulled me to my feet. Blair began to unbutton my shirt, undeterred by my jovial protests. The crowd became even more rowdy as Roslyn pulled Adrienne over to the table.

They managed to get my shirt off, but I put up a fight over the bra. A good-natured wrestling match ensued, and before I knew it I was flat on my back on the table, naked from the waist up. Roslyn and Lacey kept a hold on Adrienne and pushed her up to the table as Leigh and Blair doused me in lime juice and tequila. Rory and Allison joined in and playfully pinned my hands over my head.

The look on Adrienne's face was priceless. It was a mixture of arousal and fear. I was wiggling and breathing so heavily that Blair kept missing my belly button with the tequila, which ran down the front of my shorts and down my sides.

"You have to lick up every drop, Adrienne," Roslyn taunted as they wrestled Adrienne out of her shirt, but she managed to keep her bra on. My heart raced as she bent over with a big grin and lapped the tequila out of my navel. Her tongue on my skin would have aroused me all the more if I hadn't been surrounded by a group of women watching our every move.

She slowly licked the juice and alcohol up the center of my chest. When she got to my breasts, her eyes met mine and sent chills down my spine. Her gaze locked on mine, she licked all around my right breast, avoiding the nipple. I had to fight to keep my hips still.

She was nearly on top of me when she took my nipple into her mouth. My hips involuntarily thrust up, and she responded by grinding into me. She switched over to my left breast and treated it the same way, but when her teeth grazed my nipple my eyes rolled up into my head and I tried counting backward from a hundred in a weak attempt to cool the desire she had ignited.

I felt the warmth of her body leave me as Roslyn pulled her away. "Okay, Adrienne, your turn." The others released me and helped me off the table. "We're going to do it a little differently with you."

Roslyn playfully pinned Adrienne's arms behind her. "Hayden, you kneel down in front of her and unzip her shorts," she instructed as she held Adrienne in place.

Between the rum and arousal, I didn't mind as they pushed me down on my knees in front of her. I shyly peered up into her eyes as I unzipped her shorts. Blair handed me a shot vial and Roslyn ordered me to slip it down the front of her underwear. I did as I was told and slipped it all the way down until just the tip of it peeked out from the waistband. Leigh squeezed lime all over Adrienne's abdomen, and I eagerly licked it off as I made my way down to the vial. Leigh put her hands on my shoulders and pushed me down onto my back on the floor. Roslyn had Adrienne kneel down and straddle my body.

Adrienne, now down on all fours, arched her back and emptied the vial into my mouth. To everyone else, it looked as though she were sitting on my face. I had reached the point that I wouldn't have minded one bit if she were, even though we were in a group of people.

The crowd applauded our little show and taunted Myra and Shelby, the most reserved of the group, until they got them to take part. I managed to find my bra, but I had no idea where my shirt went. When I got my bra on, Leigh led me over to Adrienne and made me straddle her lap, facing her. "If either of you move from that spot, we'll make you do shots again," she slurred triumphantly.

Adrienne looked into my eyes, and I decided to do exactly what I wanted. I kissed her, sucking her bottom lip in between mine. I nipped her lip before slipping my tongue deep into her mouth; she responded eagerly to the kiss and pulled me tighter against her.

When we broke the kiss, Adrienne whispered, "Let's get out of here." As we stood to leave, Roslyn and Lacey thwarted our discreet escape.

"It's too early to turn in for the night," Roslyn said. "Where are you two going?"

"Um, the bathroom?" Adrienne lied.

"We have to go too." Roslyn took Lacey by the hand. She gestured toward the bathroom. "After you."

"Okay, we want to be alone. Are you satisfied?" Adrienne said as she rolled her eyes.

"It's too early to turn in for the night. It's only ten. Come with me, I have an idea." Roslyn led Lacey to the kitchen with us trailing hesitantly behind.

Once we were inside the darkened kitchen, she stopped and pushed Lacey against the counter. She laughed and said, "Didn't you ever make out at parties with your friends in the same room?"

"I have something more in mind than just making out," Adrienne responded mischievously.

"You can do that here too." Roslyn cupped Lacey's breast through her shirt. "We won't bother you, we'll be busy ourselves."

I was pretty well drunk and was finding it hard to keep my hands off Adrienne. I stood behind her and nibbled between her shoulders as she contemplated Roslyn's offer. She grabbed my hand and led me over to the counter just a few feet from where the other couple stood. I leaned against the counter as Adrienne kissed me.

She was still only clad in her bra, which I unfastened and let fall from her shoulders. As I rolled her nipple between my thumb and forefinger, her breathing became heavier. She moaned as she kissed me, sending chills up and down my spine. After unzipping my shorts, she slid them down my hips until they fell to the floor. She wasted no time slipping her hand into my underwear and entered me in one stroke.

I broke the kiss and gasped as she added another finger and began to move into me as I wrapped my arms around her neck and hung on to her to keep from falling. She bit and kissed my neck, and I turned my head to the side, giving in to her touch. Opening my eyes, I noticed Roslyn watching us as she bent Lacey over the counter.

Adrienne glanced over at them before sliding another finger into me, making me lose interest in them altogether. I buried my face against her neck as she increased her pace. Her saying "Come for me, Hayden," was all it took, and my orgasm hit me with such intensity I groaned loudly into her neck. As she stilled her fingers, I could feel my insides contracting around them.

I laid my head on her chest, gathering my strength back, and we watched Lacey and Roslyn. Roslyn teased her to the brink of insanity, letting her get close and then backing off a bit. Lacey whimpered and panted as her lover massaged her clit and filled her at the same time. Roslyn glanced over at us and smiled as Lacey begged her not to stop. It was obvious she relished the pleasure of dominating Lacey, having her completely at her mercy.

She leaned down and whispered something into Lacey's ear that we could not hear, but that caused her to groan. Lacey's legs trembled even though most of her weight was on the counter. Roslyn picked up her pace again, and this time Lacey's entire body shook as her orgasm claimed her. She screamed so loud that I wondered if the others had heard her over the music.

Adrienne would not allow me to touch her the way I wanted to. "Let's finish this later when we're alone," she whispered, breathing heavily into my ear.

When Lacey had regained her strength we went back into the bar. Adrienne and I had every intention of making a hasty retreat to her cottage, but Leigh spotted the four of us and asked where we had been. Roslyn whispered something in her ear and she smiled. Myra and Shelby caught us and demanded that we stay. They shoved drinks into our hands, and Myra dragged Adrienne onto the dance floor.

As I watched them, I realized my mouth was completely dry. I drank every drink poured for me and silently wondered if I would be an alcoholic by the time these women left the island. When Adrienne and Myra finally returned, I was so drunk I could barely walk. Needless to say, Adrienne and I never got around to our unfinished business that night.

The next morning, I woke up feeling like I had been in a fight and had been beaten over the head repeatedly with a board. Adrienne was sitting on a chair near the bed, sipping iced tea and grinning ear to ear. She spoke softly. "I bet you're feeling really bad right about now."

I moaned in agreement. I got up and staggered into the bathroom. When I returned, she was kind enough to have poured me a glass of tea, which I drank down in a few gulps. "Adrienne, those women are trying to kill us," I whimpered.

An hour, one piece of toast, and a pitcher of tea later, I began to feel human again. We lay back down on the bed and talked for a while as the aching in my head started to subside. "That was kind of freaky last night with Roslyn and Lacey. I wonder why she was so insistent that we stay with them," I said, watching Adrienne's face redden.

"That's kind of my fault, I'm afraid," she confessed meekly. "Last year when they were here, Roslyn, Leigh, and I stayed up late drinking. We shared all of our fantasies. Mine was to do it in front of someone I knew. I didn't want our first time to be in front of someone, but when you started to kiss my back I lost control. She was just helping me live out that fantasy."

"Oh?" I rolled over onto my side and faced her. "What other fantasies do you have in that head of yours?"

"I fully intend on living all of them out with you, Hayden." She smiled. "Right now, though, we have to shower and dress. We leave for Nassau soon."

Later that morning, half the group took the charter plane over to Nassau. The other half stayed behind to enjoy the beach. I was dismayed to find that Dana, as well as her roommate Katie, would be accompanying us. I couldn't prove it, but I felt like Katie had come along to keep me busy so that Dana could try and get her mitts on Adrienne.

My suspicions were confirmed when we made arrangements for cabs to take us to the market. Dana quickly hustled Adrienne into one cab while Katie pulled me into another. In the interest of our guests and not making an ass of myself, I grinned and made the best of it. But if Dana could have read my thoughts, she would have run for the hills.

Once we made it to the crowded market, Dana stuck to like a parasite. I hoped that Adrienne would break away from her and come to me, but when she didn't my jealousy intensified. I began to wonder if I was being played.

"Hayden, come look at this." Leigh picked up a wooden carving of a dolphin.

I left Katie to the straw hats she was trying on and joined her. Leigh lowered her voice. "I think Dana is really hitting on Adrienne."

I was relieved that someone else had noticed and that I wasn't just being paranoid. However, it made me that much angrier that the others had noticed it too. "I think Katie's job is to keep me occupied so that Dana can have Adrienne all to herself," I said, trying to keep my facial expression neutral.

"There's nothing more appealing to her than a woman who belongs to another. It's the thrill of the hunt for her kind," Leigh hissed. As we watched, Dana guided Adrienne through the market with her arm linked possessively through Adrienne's.

"I know that you and Adrienne have to be cordial to all the guests, but she's taking this a little too far. Do you want me to say something to her?" Leigh asked, puffing her chest out, obviously pissed.

I had to laugh at the little spitfire. "No, Adrienne's a big girl. She's free to make up her mind about what she wants." But in my mind I told myself that if she chose that over me after the previous night, when these guests left for the States I would be with them.

Katie left me alone after she noticed that Leigh and I had paired off. I carried all of Leigh's purchases as she shopped. She bought with reckless abandon, explaining that she had many people back home to buy for. All the while, I stole glances at Adrienne and her companion as they walked around the market.

Fortunately, Adrienne had a friend who worked the desk of one of the local hotels, and he agreed to store our packages while we toured the island. My arms and back were grateful.

We were lucky enough to catch a tour bus that took us to Paradise Island. I made no attempt to sit with Adrienne, choosing Leigh's company instead. Two could play this game.

To my delight we were let out near the Pizza Hut, and everyone readily agreed to go for pizza. Normally, I did not care for the taste of beer, but when Leigh ordered a couple of pitchers I decided to indulge. Combined with the pizza, the ice-cold beer was very enjoyable, but it did little to cool my anger toward Dana and Katie. If they were so hard up, why didn't they just get together?

We spent the rest of the day browsing through shops, frequently stopping for beer breaks. On the short flight back to the island, I slept, happy to forget about the events of the day.

When we arrived at the inn, dinner was being served in the dining room. Sarah had already begun to set up the bar. I was satisfied that everything was being handled and my assistance was not needed. I returned to my cottage, where I dropped headlong across the bed and drifted back to sleep. The night's festivities would have to go on without me, and considering the way Dana and Adrienne had chummed up, I doubted I would be missed. I would have had myself a full-blown pity party had sleep not claimed me first.

I was awakened sometime later by a loud knock on my door. A very pissed-off Adrienne stalked into my room. "What the hell is your problem, Hayden? You left me alone to entertain all of the guests, not to mention the fact that you basically ignored me all day!"

"You didn't need my help with the guests, Adrienne! The staff is more than capable of tending to their needs. Besides, from the look of it you had someone to keep you company!"

"Well, considering how chummy you and Katie were today—"

"Don't you try and turn this around on me, Adrienne! You know good and damn well that Dana has been following you around like a dog in heat, and even after what we discussed yesterday you entertained her today! She latched onto you like a leech and you didn't do a blessed thing to discourage her.

And don't give me that shit about needing to be nice for the guests!" I hissed, trying to keep my voice down.

"Maybe I needed to know that I was worth fighting for, Hayden," Adrienne said softly as she sat down on the bed. "No, that's wrong. I guess I just wanted to know the depth of your feelings for me. I hoped you would come and rescue me from her. I needed that reassurance from you. I went about it the wrong way today, and I'm sorry."

Even though she had apologized, I still seethed with anger, but I could feel a blanket of guilt starting to cover my frustration. "Do you have any idea what a fool you made me look like? Yesterday, we walked hand in hand, not to mention what happened in the bar last night, and today you're arm and arm with Dana. I have doted over you like a heartsick teenager almost since the minute I arrived here—and you need reassurance? Adrienne, you have the ability to see into my thoughts. Why would you need to be reassured?"

"I can hear your thoughts...sometimes. I don't always trust what I hear—it might be wishful thinking on my part. I need to see it in your actions, and I need to hear you say what I mean to you. I was wrong to do that to you. How many times do I need to say it, Hayden?" She looked up at me, and I could feel myself weakening. Guilt had definitely overtaken me.

"What do you want from me, Adrienne? I'm crazy about you. This place is beautiful, and I enjoy being here, but you're the reason I stayed."

It was that simple. That was all she needed to hear. She jumped up off the bed and pulled me into a tight hug. I felt all my anger and jealousy fade away at that moment.

Exhausted from the outing at the market and from the tense emotions we'd bottled up all day, we curled up next to each other. I drifted off as she ran her fingers though my hair. Believe it or not, all we did that night was sleep.

CHAPTER SIX

The next morning, Adrienne and I joined the group for breakfast. Dana was, of course, planted in her usual spot, but I chose to stake claim to my territory. I pulled out my usual seat and bowed low, gesturing for Adrienne to sit. I leaned down and kissed her, then took the seat next to Dana. Leigh did not even try to hide her chuckle.

"Why have we never gone diving in the blue holes before?" Donna asked around a mouth full of bacon.

"Because the local dive shops don't want to take us and that means we have to pack all of the dive equipment through the brush. You don't remember that from last year?" Shelby asked.

Iris placed a fresh platter of bacon on the table in front of Donna, then squared her shoulders and propped her hands on her hips. When she spoke, her accent was even more pronounced than usual. "Blue holes be bad, very bad tings. Creatures dat can swallow down a whole mon, even gobble up a whole big hoss, dey be livin' in dem blue holes. No, very bad ting you girls goin' over yonder."

"What kind of creatures?" Allison asked.

"Bad tings, missy. Many people try to know de secret of de holes. And dey jes up an vanish, poof dey gone. Blue holes be a bad ting. You stay clear," she warned. A hush had fallen over the room, and when I heard Iris muttering a prayer as she went back in the kitchen, a shiver ran up my spine.

"We can't keep coming here and not explore one of the island's most interesting anomalies." With that said, Donna polished off the last of her pancakes.

"I wouldn't advise diving in Bad Hole," Adrienne said. "Visibility is greatly limited because of the murky water. Island folklore tells of some sort of large creature that lives there. It may very well be a huge shark, but I wouldn't recommend trying to find out firsthand. Besides, the woods surrounding Bad Hole are full of fruit bats."

"Where is this Boiling Hole I've heard of?" Chelsey asked as she swiped a piece of bacon from Donna's plate. Chelsey, Donna's lover, was one of the sexist women at the table aside from Adrienne. I watched as she tucked her short hair behind her ears, and for a moment I pictured her in a courtroom wearing one of those smart-looking business suits. Coupled with the wire-rimmed glasses she wore, she looked incredible in my mind's eye. Adrienne interrupted my ponderings by clearing her throat; when I glanced over at her she was looking at me with an eyebrow raised.

I shrugged sheepishly. *Damnit! I forgot she can she see what's in my head.* When I looked back at her she nodded with a smug expression.

"Boiling Hole is probably a better choice than Bad Hole. You can access it by kayak or canoe. I can make arrangements for you if you like."

"Why don't you and Hayden come with us? It'll be fun. We'll snorkel so we won't have to pack in a ton of gear," Shelby said with a grin, and the whole gang joined in pleading with us to go.

It sounded like fun to me, but Adrienne rolled her eyes when I volunteered us to go along, then went to make the arrangements while I went off to get the snorkeling gear.

Iris, looking very serious, caught me by the arm on my way out. "Anyting happen to my Adrienne, I kill you." She drove her point home by waving a black iron skillet at me. If she was half as good with that skillet as she was with a wooden spoon, I didn't want to take any chances, and I assured her that Adrienne would return safe and sound or I would throw myself off Mt. Alvernia. She did not seem to find humor in that. As I went to change into my swimsuit, I wondered if this was a good idea after all.

After everyone changed and gathered their gear, we met in the bar. The van Adrienne had called for arrived, and we all helped the porters load the equipment and ice chests.

"Okay, everyone who wears sunscreen go ahead and put it on now. Do not get into the van yet." Adrienne grinned as she spoke. "There's one more thing we have to do before we leave."

We all began to smear ourselves with sunscreen. I had the enjoyable task of rubbing it into several well-toned backs. But I also made sure that I was the one to apply Adrienne's, giving Dana my best menacing glance in the process. I especially enjoyed rubbing it into her lower back and went a little farther south than she counted on, earning me a playful slap.

Rory gave voice to the question we all wanted to ask. "Why do we have to put our sunscreen on now?"

"It's best to let the sunscreen soak into your skin for thirty minutes before getting into the sun. If I tried to make this group wait thirty minutes before heading out, you'd all find a bar and be drunk before we ever made the canoe trip. You bunch of lushes," Adrienne chided.

After we were all greased up, we looked at Adrienne expectantly, waiting for what came next. "The creek that we will canoe down to Boiling Hole is lined with mangrove trees, which harbor many annoying insects. If anyone is allergic to insect repellent let me know now, because I'm about to spray you all down."

I could hear the yelps and squeals as cool repellent hit warm skin. Adrienne took great pleasure in spraying each member of the group. When it came my turn she looked at me with an evil grin. She coated the front of my body liberally with the spray, and when I turned she did the same to my back. I got an unexpected surprise when she pulled the back of my swimsuit down and sprayed the crack of my ass. I had plans to retaliate, but she tossed the repellent to Shelby. There was no way I was wrestling that giant of a woman for the can, and Adrienne knew it.

We crammed ourselves into the van, which was interesting considering we were covered in oil. I'm sure anyone seeing us had to find it amusing. The inside of the van was wall-to-wall greasy womanflesh reeking of coconut oil.

"Hey, Adrienne, is that repellent edible, because I just ate some," Rory said with an ear-to-ear grin. Allison was rubbing her shoulder where Rory had obviously nipped her. "I don't think I got enough to poison myself, but it will probably give me gas."

"You can't blame that on repellent, stinky Pete," Allison joked.

"Too much information! Have mercy!" Myra howled with laughter. "If we smell anything bad while we're crammed like sardines on this bus, you're getting an ass whipping, Rory!"

Rory and Allison were the ones whose names I had the most trouble with. They both had the same short hairstyle, though Rory's was blonde and Allison's light brown. And both always sported ball caps.

Lacey was perched on Roslyn's lap next to Adrienne and me. She looked at us in amusement. "Can we officially consider you two an item now?"

"Yes," Adrienne and I answered in unison. The entire van erupted in cheers, except of course for Dana, who sat red-faced, glaring straight ahead.

I stared out of the windows at the small plots of farmland we passed and marveled at how antiquated they all seemed. People were harvesting fruits and vegetables by hand, and some sold them at small stands on the roadway. The sight reinforced what I already knew: I was living in a much simpler world. Surprisingly, I had begun to like it.

We arrived at an inn run by a couple who knew Adrienne well and who had already made preparations for our arrival.

After a short visit, we filled the canoes two by two and started down the creek toward Boiling Hole. Adrienne and I led the group since she had made the trip a few times before.

Thick tangles of mangroves bordered both sides of the creek, casting deep shadows on the water and making it look dark and creepy. An occasional patch of sunlight revealed the clarity of the water. We were able to see all sorts of marine life below us as we paddled on.

"Um, Adrienne, did I hear you right back at the inn, that bats live in these mangroves?" I asked as we paddled down the shaded creek.

"Many creatures make their homes in the mangroves, including fruit bats. Unless you smear yourself in fruit, you shouldn't have anything to worry about."

I made a mental note to attach fruit to the straw hat that Dana was sporting. "So, um, what other creatures live in the mangroves?" I tensed up and started to study the shrubby trees more closely.

"All sorts of insects and birds. Reptiles and fish are especially fond of hiding in the mangroves' roots, which grow into the water. The roots are a safe haven from predators. When we get into a clearing you'll be able to see plenty of aquatic life peeking out from the roots." Even with my back to her, I could tell Adrienne was grinning ear to ear.

"When you say reptiles, you mean snakes, don't you?" I said as my skin began to crawl.

"Yes, all sorts of species. Hayden, if we should see a snake, do not do anything rash. Just remain calm. You don't want to capsize us and dump us into the creek with them."

"Adrienne, I can assure you that if I see a snake I will walk on water and be in the bar waiting on you and the group to get back!"

Our convoy of canoes fortunately had no problems navigating the gentle creek. I was thankful for the bug repellent that Adrienne had sprayed us down with because there were all sorts of winged insects looking for a good meal. I was careful not to swat at anything for fear of pitching Adrienne and me into the water. I had no desire to mingle with the critters.

Boiling Hole looked to me like a fresh-water pond. The water was crystal clear and very inviting even though I knew it was home to creatures real and imagined.

"Why is the water bubbling like that? Is it hot?" Lacey asked as she slowly dipped her toe into the churning water.

"It has to do with the tide. I don't think anyone really knows for sure. Island folklore says that there are mystic creatures in the holes, as well as mermaids." Adrienne cocked a brow and lowered her voice for dramatic flair. "Most islanders refuse to come anywhere near here."

Donna was the first to hit the water. When she wasn't eaten or even nibbled by any creatures, we followed her lead and jumped in. The clarity of the water afforded us a great view of the sea life that seemed totally unafraid of our presence. Even the manta ray pups swam gracefully by, brushing our legs with their tiny wings.

Some of the women who were a lot braver than I went in search of the more menacing creatures rumored to inhabit the hole. I climbed out, choosing to enjoy the sun for a while with Blair and Allison. I couldn't resist watching Adrienne's cute little bottom sticking out of the water while she snorkeled. I wondered what it would be like to dig my nails into those firm cheeks as she lay naked between my legs. I was lost in lustful thought when a voice called me back from my happy place.

"Is there anything in those coolers besides sodas?" Blair asked, eyeing one of many ice chests we'd brought with us.

"You mean like food or alcohol?" I asked.

"I mean like alcohol," she said with a grin. Her blue eyes twinkled with mischief, making her freckles look even cuter.

I got up and dragged a red ice chest over to where we were sunbathing. "I hope you like wine coolers. Seems that's all we have in this one."

When the rest of the group noticed us digging into the chests, they quickly gave up their search for the sea monster and joined us. No one seemed interested in the food since most of them had been adhering to a strict rum diet since arriving on the island. Needless to say, they quickly emptied one cooler and were delighted to find that thoughtful Adrienne had filled another with rum and fruit juice.

Some of my fondest romantic episodes had occurred near the beach when I was younger. Now whenever I'm near the water and I get a whiff of suntan oil, I get downright frisky. That is exactly why I invited Adrienne to take a stroll with me. A romantic interlude on a beach towel in some secluded spot was just what I had in mind as I grabbed her hand and led her away from the group. You can imagine how surprised I was when Adrienne and I walked up on Blair and Leigh, who obviously had the same idea.

They were so into each other that neither of them noticed us gawking at them. Hands and bodies moved in perfect unison as they pleasured each other in reckless abandon. When a huge bug nearly flew into my gaping mouth, I came to my senses and we made a hasty retreat.

We scampered to an outcropping of rocks near the water, where we both chuckled in embarrassment. Adrienne leaned against the rocks and pulled me to her. I wrapped my arms around her neck and in a matter of seconds found myself kissing her passionately. The only sounds around us were the distant voices of our friends, an occasional seagull, and our labored breathing coupled with soft moans as we kissed.

I had been craving this woman since I had met her. The wine cooler and the smell of suntan oil on the breeze drove me from frisky to downright horny. I broke away from the kiss and wove my fingers through her damp hair as I nibbled her neck. She tilted her head back, giving me full permission to continue.

I ran my fingertips over her breasts, lightly smiling against her mouth as I felt them react to my touch. I kissed her again, gently sucking her tongue into my mouth. I unfastened the clasp to her swimsuit top, never breaking the kiss while I slipped the straps off her shoulders and let the top fall to the ground.

She shuddered, and her skin broke out in goose bumps as I lightly ran my nails down her stomach. She laced her fingers through my hair this time, pulling my head back so she could kiss my neck. The sensation of her mouth on my skin at the same time my hand slipped between her legs drove me to the brink of insanity.

When she finished lavishing my neck with kisses, I could not resist the temptation and dipped my head down to circle her nipple with my tongue. She moaned and pulled me closer as I sucked and nibbled her breast and stroked her through her wet swimsuit bottom.

I suppose every drop of blood vacated my brain and went rushing south of my belly button, which would explain what happened next. The smell of suntan oil was in the air. I had a slight buzz from the single wine cooler that I had consumed, and I had Adrienne nearly naked and was pawing at her like a wild bear.

I was completely consumed by what I was doing and only slightly aware of something rubbing against my heel. Seconds later, I felt the same sensation on the other heel. All movement came to a stop. I released my lip-lock on Adrienne's breast and looked down. There behind my feet was a snake about four feet long.

What happened next was a blur, but Adrienne says I let out one of those shrill girly screams that had her ears ringing for a week. Then she said I did some exotic dance for which she had no words to describe. This in turn scared the snake, which bit me just above the ankle, and I passed out, hitting my head on the rocks.

I woke up in a hospital in Nassau with a mild concussion. Adrienne was by my side. She explained that the snake was not poisonous, but they had admitted me for observation. Most of my body was covered in scrapes and bruises from when I had passed out and slid down the rocky embankment.

I was not satisfied until I had ripped off the sheet and looked at my lower leg to make sure it was not rotting off, full of snake venom. There was just a puffy patch of red skin around the bite. I sighed with relief and fell back onto the bed, wincing from the multiple strawberry marks on my back and the stabbing pain in my head.

"Oh, dear Lord in heaven! Adrienne, I am so embarrassed." I slung an arm over my face.

"Don't be, Hayden. I would have freaked out too if I had been bitten. The gang went back to the inn after we knew you were out of danger. Iris and the staff are taking good care of them. The really good news is the doctor is releasing you this morning," Adrienne said as she stroked my hair.

"This morning? How long have I been here, for Pete's sake?" I whimpered after raising my voice and sending shock waves through my head.

"They kept you last night just to be on the safe side. Besides, you were pretty much out of it." Adrienne handed me a T-shirt and a pair of shorts that one of the girls had loaned us.

She helped me out of my hospital gown, kindly looking away to preserve my dignity while I slipped commando into someone else's shorts. I was barely able to lift my arms to pull the shirt over my head due to the abrasions on my elbows. Adrienne gently tugged the shirt down over my head and helped me with the sleeves. Once she had brushed the knots out of my hair, she put it up in a ponytail. I managed to wash my own face and began to feel human again, even though I didn't smell like one.

I tugged at the shorts that were two sizes too small and left my ass cheeks exposed to the world while Adrienne was kind enough to do the paperwork associated with checking me out of the hospital. I swallowed hard when I saw all of the medications the nurse handed to her, giving instructions for each. She stuffed them into a bag and gave me a little grin before waving me over to sign the last of the papers.

"What's in the bag?" I asked as we climbed into a cab.

Adrienne smiled as she recited the list. "Some ointment for the bite site itself, oral antibiotics which are quite strong, and something for a yeast infection that the nurse said you'll surely get after taking the meds."

"Oh, that just puts the icing on the cake, doesn't it?" I groaned.

"Let me cheer you up by telling you what happened to me after you and the snake got up close and personal." Adrienne draped an arm over my shoulders. "When you began to scream and dance around, the others came running. By the time they made it to us, you were lying on the ground unconscious and I was standing there topless. You have no idea the jokes I had to endure about my tits scaring you half to death."

I couldn't help but chuckle. "Actually, you have the nicest pair I've had the pleasure of—" I was interrupted by the cab driver clearing his throat and reminding us of his presence.

When we arrived back on the island, one of the porters was kind enough to be waiting at the airstrip for us. I dreaded going back to the inn and facing the women who I knew would rib me about this for the rest of the trip. Had this happened to anyone else, I would have shown them no mercy. And I expected no less from those women.

"Hayden, when we get back to the inn we're going straight to my cottage and you're taking a hot, soaking bath. When you're done, you will lie in the bed watching TV or reading for the day. I want you to relax so your body will heal quickly. Iris, the staff, and I will be able to take care of the girls with no problems."

I agreed to do just that. My skin burned from the abrasions, and I ached from head to toe. A nice bath was just what I needed.

Once we arrived at the inn, a large herd of laughing lesbians surrounded the vehicle. They helped Adrienne pull me from the van and walk me into the bar, where I stood stiffly as they told me the story of how they got me from the Boiling Hole to the neighboring inn.

"Aren't you glad I brought an extra pair of shorts and a shirt with me?" Chelsey said with a smile.

"Yes, I am. They came in very handy, but I regret to inform you that I'm not wearing any underwear. I'll have to owe you a new pair." I tugged them down over my backside.

"In that case, you're welcome to keep them. Consider it a get-well gift." She chuckled.

Adrienne walked me back to her cottage, and after my bath I climbed into her bed feeling refreshed and relaxed. Adrienne took a shower and joined me, saying she hadn't slept very well in the chair in my hospital room. I felt terrible hearing that. She probably was feeling much worse than I was but had never uttered one complaint.

Sarah woke us up when she brought dinner. She was smiling ear to ear, sporting the shirt I had given her.

"Sarah, that shirt looks better on you than it ever did me. Would you like to join us for dinner? I'm sure Iris sent enough to feed a small army," I said, trying to shift my weight to a body part that did not ache.

"I can't tonight. I'm helping out in the bar."

"That's my fault and I'm sorry, Sarah. I hope we're not keeping you from anything you wanted to do," I said, feeling guilty for her having to work in my place.

"No problem at all. I'm having a great time with the girls. One has been very nice to me. I think her name is Dana."

When she left us, Adrienne chuckled. "If Dana thinks she's going to get lucky with Sarah, she has another thing coming. Iris thinks of her as a daughter and will break Dana in half."

I attempted to get out of bed and was met by an angry glare.

"Don't even think about getting out of that bed, Hayden. You're staying off your feet all day." She settled a little tray over my lap and put a plate full of Mexican food on it.

"Iris does it all, doesn't she? Mexican, Italian—this woman is my hero!" I took a bite, and the fresh guacamole made my eyes tear in pure pleasure. "These enchiladas are a slice of heaven! I may have to ask Iris to marry me." Adrienne shot me an indignant look as she filled her own plate.

"So, did I ruin everyone else's trip to the Boiling Hole?" I asked between bites.

"No, the gang was almost ready to go anyway. Fortunately, Dr. Shelby and Medic Donna knew what to do until we got you to where we could call for help. Shelby tended to you while Myra and I paddled the canoe. My arms are still sore trying to move all of that weight back down the creek."

"Adrienne, I'm so sorry, baby. I know I shouldn't have panicked, but that...that creature touched me. I freaked." I was losing my appetite, knowing the trouble I had caused.

"You don't need to apologize. Just having you back here safe and sound is all that matters to me. I was so afraid that we weren't going to get you to the hospital in time. Myra and Shelby were quick to kill the snake so we could take it to the hospital. You can't imagine my relief when the doctors confirmed that it wasn't poisonous. Although, when you woke up in the ER and started screaming snake at the top of your lungs, I nearly wet my pants."

As Adrienne ran another hot bath for me, there was a knock at the door. She opened it to the combined force of ten alcohol-laced lesbians, who piled into our cottage. "We missed you guys, so we came to check on you," Rory babbled, obviously drunk, with her hat on sideways.

Shelby ushered me over to the bed and demanded to check my bite. I, of course, had no intention of arguing with a woman who towered over me like a giant. She gently pulled the bandage off the wound and requested peroxide and the ointment the hospital had sent home with me.

"Um, Shelby, I was just about to take a bath. Do you mind if we do this when I get out?" I looked up at all of the faces peering over her shoulder.

"Sure, Monkey Chops, but don't forget. This can get infected very easily if you don't take care of it."

"Where are Dana and Katie?" Adrienne asked when she noticed they were not part of the group.

"Well, Katie decided to keep Dana company since she didn't feel very comfortable coming with us. Seems she's still a tad upset about what Hayden said yesterday," Leigh said with a giggle.

"Oh, I'm gonna go get the peroxide," Adrienne said as she quickly left the room.

"What did I say to Dana? I really don't remember talking to her yesterday."

"You don't remember it because you were semiconscious and talking out of your head." Myra patted me on the shoulder. "You didn't offend us, but Dana was a little put off." The entire room broke out in raucous laughter.

"Come on, y'all. For the love of Pete, tell me what I said."

Adrienne returned to the room looking a little guilty. She knew I wanted to choke her for leaving this tidbit out.

"We couldn't understand most of what you said, but we were able to make out the part about Dana being a ho and you wishing a fruit bat would eat her," Leigh said between snorts of laughter.

I couldn't hold back. I laughed right along with them in my embarrassment. Well, at least I hadn't voiced what I really felt about her. Words that would make a sailor blush ran through my mind when I thought about that woman.

After the gang left us for their nightly routine of skinny-dipping, Adrienne helped me into the bath. "This is not how I wanted you to see me naked for the first time." I sighed as she gingerly washed my back, which had sustained most of the damage from my fall.

"Actually, this isn't the first time I've seen you naked," Adrienne confessed.

"It was dark the night we skinny-dipped. You didn't see much."

"No, I saw you naked when they admitted you into the hospital last night. They had stripped you of your wet swimsuit and covered you with a blanket when you were brought in. When you woke up and started screaming about the snake, you jerked the blanket off and half of the ER got a prime view."

"Oh, this just gets better by the minute! Please tell me, did I bust out into a chorus of show tunes at any time?"

Adrienne lost all composure and laughed until she cried. I simply sat there staring at her angrily until she regained control of herself. Maybe now Carla and her linebacker girlfriend had forgotten about me and I could safely return to the States. I was never going to live this down.

Invigorated by my bath, I decided to reward Adrienne with a well-deserved back rub. She lay across the bed as I massaged lotion into her back and arms. Her soft moans reminded me of the previous day, before that devil in a snakeskin paid me a visit. As arousing as it was, I couldn't physically do anything about it because even my hair still ached. Soft snores stirred me from my ponderings, and I looked down to find Adrienne already asleep.

The next morning I felt much better and spent quality time with Saber while Adrienne slept. "Next time I go anywhere on this island, you have to accompany me and protect me from the slimy kind," I said as I stroked his orange fur. He purred delightedly at all the attention.

I took the tip of his little orange tail and ran it lightly over Adrienne's nose. Her brow furrowed and her nose twitched, but she didn't wake up. Undaunted, I tried another approach. I took Saber's tail and ran it lightly down her arm. She grumbled and scratched and then flipped over on her other side. It was time to pull out the big gun. I gently lifted one of her long locks of hair and dragged it across the bed. Of course this was too much temptation for a feline, and he had to pounce. As we say in Louisiana, I got a fussin'. Mission accomplished—she was awake.

Adrienne and I dressed and went to the dining room to have breakfast with the girls. If looks were daggers, I'd have been sliced to shreds with the glare Dana threw at me when we entered the room. I must have been living right that morning because she completely ignored me throughout the meal. This pleased me to no end.

"So, Hayden, tell us the truth. Did you pass out when you saw Adrienne's breasts for the first time, then blame it on the snake?" Allison asked, and the room broke out into hysterical laughter.

"They are they loveliest pair I've ever seen," I retorted. "I didn't actually pass out 'til I touched them."

"Well, we have to agree with you there, because we all saw them!" Roslyn said, laughing hysterically.

I had never seen Adrienne turn that shade of crimson before. I was glad she was taking it on the chin right along with me. We could hardly eat because all of the jokes being thrown at us.

In the heat of the day, most of the gang went down to the beach to swim. Shelby and Myra joined Adrienne and me in the bar.

"Adrienne, I've been thinking about the view of the beach from the guest cottages," I said as I sipped my tea.

She glanced at me as if I were insane. "There is no view. It's all grown up with banana plants and brush. We've always been afraid to cut it because of erosion."

"That's precisely what I'm talking about. The view from the bluff is magnificent and shouldn't be obstructed. I think we can get rid of some of the higher brush and trees and plant something low profile in there that will live in that sandy soil. That way the guests will have a view of the water." To illustrate my plan, I drew little sketches on a cocktail napkin.

Adrienne nodded. "We'd have to wait until our guests go home before undertaking a task like that. I agree, though, it would add to the beauty of the inn."

About that time, Shelby jumped in. "Since you guys brought it up, Myra and I would like to talk to you about staying on here for a few more weeks. Of course we'll pay for our cottage and help you with the land clearing, should you agree."

"Don't you have to return to your practice, Shelby?" Adrienne asked. She sounded as surprised as I was by the change of events.

"That's the other thing we'd like to discuss with you. I'm tired of my practice back home. I've been considering selling for a while, but I'm nowhere near retirement age. Myra and I have been very frugal with our spending and have managed to pay off all of our debts. The other day when Hayden got hurt showed me there is a real need for a doctor here. If that had been a poisonous snake, the outcome might have been dire, considering how long it took us to get to Nassau. It made me think about how wonderful it would be to open a practice here. I could feel like I was truly helping people again."

"I am sure Hayden feels the same as I do—we'd love to have you here, but surely you've noticed that much of the island is impoverished and probably can't sustain much. Our medical clinic struggles to keep up with the demand as it is."

Myra piped up. "Shelby and I have discussed that too. When we return to the States, we plan on seeing what we can do for additional funding. We know a few doctors who are excellent at organizing fund-raising campaigns for small clinics in other countries that need help updating their medical programs."

"It seems like you two have definitely thought this over, and you seem to know what you'd be getting into. I'll do whatever I can to help make this happen. Besides, I can't imagine two people I'd enjoy more living on this island. Don't even consider trying to pay us for the extended stay. If you help us with the land clearing, then consider your debt paid," Adrienne said with a grin.

After a friendly argument about debts, Myra and Shelby agreed to Adrienne's offer. I was thrilled to have them stay with us, not to mention that it would be very comforting to have a physician on hand.

CHAPTER SEVEN

Since Adrienne would let me do little else, I spent the remainder of the day hobbling around gathering up the supplies that I thought we would need to undertake my project. The gang had decided to take it easy and hang around the inn, so I took full advantage of the van and went into New Bight, the island's biggest town.

Saber accompanied me and did well on the ride. He lay across my lap as I drove and behaved as though he had been riding in a vehicle for years. That is, until I was reminded that I was no longer in New Orleans and the Bahamians drove on the left side of the road. Me and a truck full of pineapples nearly collided head-on. I jerked the wheel, causing Saber to dig is claws into my thighs and hang on for dear life. Ya know, the middle finger really is a universal gesture.

I managed to find something resembling a hardware store and left Saber to sleep on the driver's seat. I left all of the windows down, and he seemed contented as the breeze tousled his orange fur.

The place was a cross between a hardware store and a grocery store. I found a few things that would help us out, but not much. The owner was happy to show me around and when I told him I was Gloria's niece, he treated me like family.

He looked me over, pointing to all of the scrapes and bruises that peppered my body, not to mention the bleeding scratches that now marked both of my thighs.

"What happened to you?"

I told him about the incident at Boiling Hole, leaving out the part about me ravishing Adrienne's gorgeous body just prior to the snakebite. His eyes widened as I relayed the details. A few others gathered around, and before long I had them all captivated with my story. They marveled at my bravery for going to such an evil place and surviving. We all sat down right in the middle of one of the aisles as several of the locals related their stories of the evil holes.

Every story I heard told of a sea creature named Lusca. One said it was half shark, half octopus. Others said it was half dragon, half octopus. However, all were in agreement on two points: Lusca lived in the blue holes on the island; and those who ventured into the water were eaten. The stories were entertaining, some even a bit scary. However, the island storytellers related each Lusca episode as if they were reporting the news. And the fear that filled their eyes and voices told me that they really believed the creature existed.

When my rear end began to protest about the hardness of the floor, I thanked my new friends and took my items to the old register.

"The holes are very bad things. Never good to go there, you are lucky to be alive," said the owner, a small bald-headed man with very dark skin and even darker eyes as he rang up my purchases. "Many people have disappeared in the holes. Don't go back."

I thanked him for his advice. Although I did not believe in the creature they spoke of, the residents of Cat Island deeply feared the holes. And while I still wondered what actually did live in that water, the locals' obvious fear made me think twice about ever going back.

Saber greeted me with sleepy little cat eyes when I returned to the van. He nestled himself back on my lap and was asleep before I got the van in gear. I was reminded yet again by one of the friendly locals to keep my ass on the left side of the road as I sped toward the inn.

I was eager to get started on the land-clearing project. I had a mental picture of how I wanted it to look, and I wanted to get my hands in the dirt once again. When I arrived at the inn, I was surprised to see Hank the pirate in the bar with Adrienne. Even more surprising, he helped me unload the supplies. When I told him all about my project, he mumbled something about having a fishing trip planned and tromped off. Silently elated, I breathed a sigh of relief; I didn't want to spend any more time around him than I had to, especially not downwind.

I grabbed an iced tea and decided to relax and smoke a cigarette before finding out what the wild tribe was up to. When I was fully relaxed and enjoying the solitude, Shelby rounded the corner and proclaimed I was just the person she wanted to see.

"Hiya, Monkey Chops!" I had no idea why Shelby's pet name for me was Monkey Chops, but I took it all in stride since I had no idea what a monkey chop was.

"Let me have a look at the—" Her voice trailed off and her eyes widened in surprise. "Whoa! Woman, what on earth happened to you?" I explained in painful detail why driving on the wrong side of the road with a cat on your lap is not a bright idea.

"I'll be right back with something for those cuts. Stay put. And don't make me hunt you, or I will use rubbing alcohol." She trotted off.

Once she had cleaned the new wounds, she focused on the snakebite. She gently removed the bandage. "This looks a little infected." She began to clean the wound. "Have you been keeping this clean?"

"Sure I have, but in this climate I've been sweating like a whore on dollar day."

She glanced up at me with her brows knitted together. "Hayden, you have quite a way with words, honey."

"Sorry, I picked that expression up from Hank. Adrienne's been following me around with peroxide and antibiotic ointment since it happened. I don't think we can get it any cleaner," I said as she poked around on it, causing me to wince in pain.

"You're a very active woman, Monkey Chops, but I think you need to take it easy for a couple of days. I would strongly suggest that you do not fool around with clearing that land until this looks better."

"I agree," Adrienne said as she came back into the bar. "Besides, you know we can't do anything until our guests leave. I don't think any of the girls want to spend their vacation in a construction zone."

I pouted, sulked, sucked my thumb, and those two would not relent. I had been put on a short leash and there was nothing I could do about it. To make matters worse, I couldn't even drown my sorrows in rum because of the antibiotics.

Adrienne tried to cheer me up, and under any other circumstances it would have worked. She ran her fingers through my hair and whispered, "Why don't you and I go back to my cottage and finish what we started the other day?"

I looked into those smoldering eyes and felt tears filling my own. "Adrienne, I can't," I whimpered pitifully. "Where exactly did you put that medicine for the yeast infection the nurse said I was sure to get? Something's not right south of my belly button." I laid my head on her shoulder.

I could feel her body trembling with laughter, but she fought it valiantly, trying to be supportive of my newly acquired condition. "Let's go back to my cottage, and I'll help you take your medicine."

"Oh, hell no! That's one thing a girl has to do by herself." Adrienne laughed so hard that she couldn't catch her breath. *This day sucks!*

Aside from Dana ruffling my feathers and my little mishap, we enjoyed our guests and the time passed quickly. The day before they were to leave they decided to hang around the inn and spend time with us. Sadness hung in the air. For them it was because the next day they would return to their everyday lives, and two of their group would still be enjoying the island. For us it was because good friends were leaving; it would be another year before they returned.

That afternoon we decided to go down to the beach and play volleyball. Couples would be divided and would play on opposing teams. My team was blessed with Dana.

I honestly did my best to behave, but when she made a remark about Adrienne's cleavage that she knew I was sure to hear, my blood began to boil. It was my turn to serve, and I could feel my hackles rise when I noticed Dana was positioned directly in front of Adrienne at the net. I knew deep down in my soul where her eyes were trained, and so I did it.

I threw the ball up and let it drop a little lower than I should for a serve. I hit that ball with all that I had. It connected with my intended target and nailed Dana in the back of the head. I, of course, should have won an Academy Award when I pretended to apologize and beg her forgiveness.

Adrienne couldn't even look at me. I could tell that she was fighting the urge to laugh. Leigh, however, didn't even try to disguise it. She laughed for fifteen minutes straight, once having to call time out so she could catch her breath. Needless to say, the rest of the gang made it a point to stay between Dana and me after that.

Dinner that evening was special. There was no big fanfare—we all sat around the table laughing at the events of the past two weeks. Shelby and Myra suffered repeated jabs for abandoning the group and staying behind on the island. We spent the evening in the bar, drinking and dancing. I didn't care to dance, so I decided to stay behind the bar and serve drinks. I had no rhythm—hell, I got confused during sex! Nevertheless, when a slow song came on, Adrienne pulled me out onto the floor with her.

The next morning we all got up early and had breakfast before the sun rose. Adrienne and I were both shocked to see the undergarments that had turned up missing the first night we'd skinny-dipped hanging all over the bar. All twelve guests had signed them before leaving them out for the world to see.

After a round of fierce ribbing, we hugged them all with the exception of one.

Adrienne, Shelby, Myra, and I waved as the vans rolled out of sight. All four of us were exhausted and unanimously agreed that going back to bed was an excellent idea.

"Do you think you can behave yourself if I nap with you?" Adrienne asked after we left the other couple and made our way through the courtyard.

"I can assure you that you'll be perfectly safe, wiseass. I'm too tired to maul you," I replied with a grin.

We returned to my cottage where Adrienne, Saber, and I climbed into bed. It was a little too warm to cuddle, so we compromised by holding hands while we slept. Saber designated himself as chaperone and curled up between us. We slept soundly for two hours before the heat started to make us restless.

Neither of us wanted to go to the trouble of bathing again just to go out and sweat, so we rolled out of bed and prepared to work. It was a good thing we decided to forgo bathing. because Hank met us in the courtyard and told us he'd cut the water off at the main line when Iris reported seeing some water puddles. We had a leak in the main sewer line between the bar and the laundry cottage.

It was odd to see a pirate with a monkey wrench. I couldn't help but stare—pirates didn't have monkey wrenches, they sported parrots. As Hank gave us a colorful rundown on the repairs, I couldn't resist conjuring up the image of a brilliantly colored parrot squawking on his shoulder.

"The old pipe is complete shit." *Complete shit, complete shit*, went the parrot. I bit my lip to keep from laughing out loud. "We're gonna have to dig a damn trench and replace the whole son of a bitch." *Damn trench, damn trench*, quoted the parrot, and I let out a chuckle. "I don't know what you think is so damned funny about that," he yelled at me, "because there's another leak where the line goes into the laundry cottage, and some poor bastard smaller than my big ass is gonna have to nut up and climb into that hole I dug and fix the main fitting." *Poor bastard, nut up, nut up,* chimed the parrot, at which point I snorted out a laugh.

Everybody looked at me as if I'd lost my mind; I just waved them off and clamped my hand over my mouth to regain my composure. Time was of the essence, after all. I looked around for a bastard smaller than Hank and came up with zip. Since I did have some limited plumbing experience from landscaping, I volunteered—reluctantly. Adrienne wasn't keen on the idea, but like me, she knew we didn't have much of a choice.

As luck would have it, Shelby and Myra had chosen that day to venture out and take a tour of the island's medical facility. Our makeshift plumbing crew consisted of the pirate, Adrienne, me, and a big black woman who threw dirt like there was no tomorrow. Whatever we were paying Iris, it wasn't enough. She went through that ground like a giant mole on speed.

It took us the better part of the day to dig up the old line. Laying the pipe for the new line was significantly easier. When it came time to seal the new pipe to the line connecting at the cottage, I wanted to cry. I had no idea why, but Hank had dug a huge and relatively deep hole around where the two pipes connected.

It was there that I learned that the old saying was in fact true: shit rolls downhill. Whatever managed to pass through the old pipe was in that hole. I found an old piece of wood to place over it. I knelt on the wood and was able to reach where I needed to work. I wasn't sure why Hank hadn't thought of that, but I assumed he hated me and wanted me knee-deep in crap.

By the time I had finished sealing the fittings, I was drooling like a dog and fighting the urge to throw up. Adrienne and Iris were kind enough to fix Hank and me a glass of iced tea. I sat in the courtyard and sipped it until my nausea passed, and decided right then that I really didn't like Hank.

"Hank, you repaired that line last year when it leaked near the laundry cottage. Why is it leaking again already?" Adrienne asked.

Hank shrugged. "Bad fitting, I guess."

I didn't know a whole lot about plumbing, but that answer sounded pretty weak. I suspected shoddy workmanship. I kept my suspicions to myself, though, because Hank, the pirate without a parrot, was still holding the pipe wrench.

Fortunately, we were able to cut the water back on and take showers. Iris had the night off, and Adrienne and I decided to have dinner at another inn operated by a friend of hers.

We took the Jeep, and to my surprise the bugs from hell that I'd encountered when I first arrived on the island had decided to stay in for the evening. Dinner at the other inn was good, but it didn't compare to Iris's cooking.

"Adrienne, do we pay Iris well?" I asked as I prepared to attack a slice of cheesecake.

"Iris makes very good money. In fact, I recently gave her a raise. She stayed mad at me for a week." Adrienne chuckled.

"Why would she be mad about getting a raise? Most people are tickled pink."

"She thinks we pay her too much. She says what she does for us is a labor of love." Adrienne went on to explain, "Her husband fell ill and died shortly thereafter. This was two years ago. Iris couldn't afford to pay her rent without his income and was evicted. Your aunt was building a little house for herself on the edge of the property. As you can guess, she gave it to Iris. Gloria couldn't stand the idea of Iris and her two children living in poverty."

I knew my aunt was a kind and generous woman, but I couldn't help but be amazed at the lengths she went to for other people. I wondered if she was the milkman's child, because my dad was nothing like that. It saddened me to think that I'd never made the effort to be closer to such a beautiful person and that it wasn't until after she'd died that I learned how amazing she truly was.

"Hayden, I need to talk to you about something, and I'm not sure how you'll react. Please promise me that you won't blow a gasket."

"Well, when you preface it like that, I can feel my steam rising already," I said, irritated that she had so little faith in me.

"The reason Hank dug the hole so big around the sewer line is because he was looking for something. He broke the line in the process. When you mentioned the land-clearing project, he got nervous and was afraid we would find what he was hiding."

"Adrienne, did he tell you this or do you just know? What the hell was he hiding?"

"No, he didn't tell me, but I'm certain he was hiding something in the ground behind the laundry cottage." She looked at me a little fearfully. She wasn't afraid of the way I would react; she was afraid I wouldn't believe her.

I took her hand. "I think we need to send old Hank packing. We can handle the repairs ourselves, and besides, he gives me the creeps. Not to mention that he smells like the south end of a northbound mule."

"I've considered that, but I'm afraid it will just make him angry. Can you imagine the havoc he could wreak on us? I've thought about this long and hard. Whatever he hid in that hole can't be good. I think we need to give this some time. Maybe we'll figure out what he's up to."

"You have a point there, dear. Okay, we keep an eye on pirate man 'til we figure out what he is up to. Let's just hope it's illegal and he'll be arrested, and the problem will be resolved." I ate the last bite of cheesecake.

It was refreshing to be out and about. We decided to ride up the coastline. The full moon lit up the sky like a beacon and made the white-capped water look like it had diamonds scattered on top of it. The air was fresh, clean-smelling. I glanced over at Adrienne and then back at the moon. Yeah, life was good in spite of it all.

When we returned to the inn, Adrienne made a quick stop at the bar and grabbed a bottle of wine and two glasses. We went back to her cottage, where we sat at her patio table and drank the wine.

I was shocked when she grabbed my cigarettes and lit one up for herself. "I didn't know you smoked," I said in surprise.

"I'm an ex-smoker. Every now and then when I have something to drink I like to have one, but I don't want to make a habit of it."

I raised a brow. "What else don't I know about you?"

"Hmm, let me see. Did you know that before I came here I entertained the idea of studying law?"

"Why did you give it up?" I asked as I refilled our glasses.

"I came here during spring break with friends. I met your aunt, and she was the closest thing to a mother that I have ever known. My mom gave me up for adoption when I was born; apparently she was an unwed mother and felt she had no other choice. My adopted parents are wonderful, but I never really established a bond with them. When it was time to go home, my heart broke at the prospect of leaving Gloria behind. I weighed the pros and cons and decided that I would be much better off here with her. She welcomed me with open arms. I've never looked back."

Adrienne's eyes misted as she talked about my aunt. "Hayden, I was so happy when you agreed to come to the island. I was comforted by that." She smiled and looked away. We sat a while in a comfortable silence, watching the moon go down, as we finished our wine.

"Would you stay with me tonight?" she asked through the darkness that had settled around us.

"You do realize that you're going to spoil me and I'm not going to want to sleep by myself anymore," I joked, but there was more truth to that statement than she knew.

Even though we had gotten pretty intimate a couple of times, I was nervous and my hands began to shake. The sexy tone in her voice told me that she wasn't interested in sleeping. I had waited for just such a moment for so long, but now my knees were knocking together under the table so hard I was afraid I wouldn't be able to walk.

When we entered her cottage she took me by the hand and led me to the bed, where she spun me around and shoved me down onto it. I lay there propped up on my elbows, staring at her. She reached under the simple summer dress she wore and slipped her panties slowly down her thighs. My heart pounded as I watched her slide out of the dress and walk toward me.

I had such a burning desire to touch and taste her that I could barely contain myself. I didn't care if she laid a hand on me, I simply wanted to please her repeatedly. She straddled my hips and pushed me completely down onto the bed, then unbuttoned my shirt. She never stopped looking into my eyes the entire time.

I ran my hands up and down the silky skin of her thighs. When she leaned over me so that her breasts were in my face, I moaned at the feel of it. I cupped them in my hands as I kissed her cleavage. She supported herself on her arms and ground her center into my stomach. I took her nipple into my mouth and she whispered, "Hayden, unbutton your shorts." Which I gladly did.

She lifted herself off me and pulled my shorts down my hips, along with my underwear. Next, she pulled me into a sitting position and took off the rest of my clothes. Gently, she pushed me back down and spread my legs with her own. She slowly rubbed her clit against mine as she kissed and bit my neck, then whispered breathlessly into my ear, "I hope you don't mind, but I have a thing about being on top."

Hell no, I didn't mind! I couldn't get enough of her. The feeling of our skin, wet with sweat, sliding so easily nearly sent me over the edge many times. She did allow me to lie fully upon her, and when she wrapped those long legs around mine I could not hold back the groan that escaped me. I dug my nails into the bed so hard as I ground my body into hers that I think I temporarily stopped the blood flow to my fingers.

She flipped me over onto my back, and I closed my eyes and basked in the pleasure of being so close to her that I had become completely unaware of anything else. I kissed and licked every inch of skin that was available to me. She slid her body up and straddled my face. I wrapped my arms around her thighs and eagerly pulled her to me. The first taste of her was exquisite. The moans and the things she said made me want to devour her, and when she finally gave in and came for me I greedily took every drop she gave.

It took her only seconds to recover and she kissed her way down my body briefly, stopping at my breasts before continuing on. She kissed the insides of my thighs and my stomach. I was not in the mood to be teased; I wove my fingers into her hair and pushed her down. She growled and sank her tongue into me. She moaned so much as she ran her tongue over me that I wondered if she was enjoying it more than I was. Then I decided that was impossible.

We were both insatiable, and we exhausted each other throughout the night. When sleep finally claimed Adrienne, she snuggled into my arms as I lay there, fingering the ends of her hair. I smiled into the darkness thinking she was exactly the lover I thought she would be. She approached making love with an intensity that was mind-blowing.

When the grayness of dawn filled our room, I closed my eyes and let sleep claim me. Later in the morning, we woke in a mass of tangled arms and legs. We lay there for a while, cuddled together.

"Hayden, I don't want to get out of bed. I wish it would rain so we wouldn't have to get up." Adrienne slipped her hand under the covers and teased my nipple, making me squirm. I grabbed her hand and kept her from moving. She frowned and tried to tug her hand free.

"Are you trying to kill me, Adrienne?" I ached from head to toe after the marathon sex we'd had the night before.

"No. I promise to make you feel really good if you let go of my hand."

How could I resist an offer like that? I freed her hand and she slid it down between my legs. My eyes fluttered shut as her skillful hand went to work, and I turned my face away from her.

"Look at me, Hayden." I opened my eyes. "Don't turn away from me. I want to watch you." She had me put my hands above my head as she stroked me. I stared into her eyes as long as I could, but they closed again as the sensation became more intense. A sudden commotion outside intruded into my reverie, forcing my eyes open again.

"Ignore it, baby, concentrate on what you feel." Her fingers inside me kept perfect time with my hips. Then she slipped them out and began to expertly massage my clit. I bit my bottom lip as she brought me closer. As I felt the first waves of my orgasm, I struggled to keep quiet.

We stayed in the bed two hours longer, morning breath and all.

CHAPTER EIGHT

The day when we would start to clear the land behind the cottages had finally arrived. First, we used machetes to chop at the banana plants that grew in abundance. Saber joined us on the job and lay lazily in the sun as we worked. I hoped that the scent of a feline would scare away any snakes that might be hiding in the brush, but my hopes were quickly dashed when Adrienne explained that the island was home to a large python population. My stomach churned at the thought that one of those wretched creatures would consider making a meal out of my pet.

Once the trees were cut away, we began the tedious task of digging out the roots. The root base was not that big, but the sheer number of stumps kept us busy the entire morning. Shelby and I did the digging while Adrienne and Myra hauled the debris away to a burn pile.

I stopped often to admire my lover as she worked. She wore nothing but a pair of cargo shorts and a sports bra. The muscles under her tanned skin bulged as she loaded the stumps onto the wagon, yet she maintained a feminine quality. I found the combination irresistible.

Shelby caught me staring as Adrienne and Myra loaded up the burn pile. "You two had quite a night last night." She grinned ear to ear.

"Yeah, dinner was really nice." I stopped to wipe the sweat from my brow.

"I'm not talking about dinner, Hayden. You two kept Myra and me awake for a while last night," she said. "I didn't figure you for a screamer, or Adrienne, for that matter, but we heard two very distinct cries coming from your cottage last night."

I stood there red-faced with my jaw hanging open. I decided it would be best not to say anything to Adrienne because I have to admit I loved hearing her scream my name. I wasn't about to say anything to discourage it.

When the heat of the day released its full fury upon us, we changed into our swimsuits and hit the beach. The coolness of the water refreshed us all and eased the ache of sore muscles. When Sarah appeared on the bluff and summoned us for lunch, we all groaned at the thought of having to climb back up the hill. Hunger won out, though, and we made the hike.

Iris served up homemade chicken salad sandwiches on flaky crescent rolls, with a side of mixed fruit. For a while, no one spoke as we ate in the coolness of the bar. After we finished eating, we rested in the chaise lounges with iced tea, whining like old women about our sore muscles.

"I think there was something living amongst those trees," Myra said. "It's been digging holes all over the place out there."

Adrienne and I exchanged glances. We had both noticed the holes as well, surrounded by fresh earth.

"You two know what's making those holes, don't you?" Shelby asked.

"It's not what, it's who," Adrienne said. "Ladies, I need to explain something to you both. This is going to sound very strange, but please give me the benefit of the doubt."

I knew what Adrienne was going to tell them, and I hoped they would react much better than I had when she'd told me. I held my breath and watched Myra and Shelby's expressions as Adrienne explained her ability to "know" things.

After she finished speaking, she looked at them, obviously expecting to be chastised. Myra was the first to speak up.

"Adrienne, that is amazing! Can you control it, or do the thoughts just come at random?"

"I have no control over it. The thoughts just pop into my head. It really comes in handy when we have new guests checking into the inn. Usually, we know what to expect before they arrive." Adrienne stole one of my cigarettes. Her hand trembled slightly as she opened the pack.

"How fascinating! Can you tell us about the next group of guests?" Shelby asked excitedly.

I noticed the dark expression that clouded Adrienne's face when she thought about the upcoming guests, just as it had when we had discussed them the previous afternoon.

"There are three lesbian couples, one of which is trying to rekindle their relationship. Another couple is simply on vacation, and the other has only been together six months. There's a husband and wife who will tell everyone they just wanted a vacation off the beaten path. They're actually looking to add another to their bed. They chose our inn because we cater to the gay and lesbian community.

"There's a gay couple as well. The more boisterous of the two is obnoxious and will make an ass of himself. His lover is often embarrassed by his mate's behavior but chooses to tolerate him. Something about these two is not right, but I can't put my finger on it.

"The last guest causes me great trepidation. Nothing comes to mind on him, but I feel very uncomfortable when I think about him. There is something wrong with this man." Adrienne trembled slightly as she said this.

Myra and Shelby actually looked frightened. "You have no idea what makes you uncomfortable about him? What if he's a serial killer or something?" Shelby asked.

"I have no idea what it is, but I do feel that he's supposed to be here for some reason. I don't feel fear toward him, I feel sadness. It's odd for someone to come here alone. Our brochures make it blatantly obvious that Gloria's Inn is more of a couples place. Because of the sadness I feel surrounding him, I've wondered if he's coming here to end his life."

"We need to make it a point to keep an eye on this guy." I lit another cigarette, which Adrienne quickly stole from my lips.

After our break, we returned to work. I had dug up some small flowering shrubs that I'd found farther up the beach. I hoped that they would take well to transplanting as I planted them in the now-barren area behind the cottages. To keep people from trampling the new plants, we interspaced some small boulders between them.

Iris joined us that afternoon and helped us line the edge of the bluff with more boulders to shield the exposed land from the winds blowing off the water. Iris amazed me; with little or no effort, she hefted boulder after boulder into place. I made a mental note: Iris was not a woman to be toyed with.

We were amazed that in one day we had managed to clear the land and replant it. Everyone agreed we would spend the next two days paying for it in sore muscles. However, the benefits outweighed the pain. The view from the cottages was spectacular, just as I had imagined, and the unimpeded breeze off the water made the cottages significantly cooler.

The following day, we moved my clothes and toiletries into Adrienne's place. Myra and Shelby moved into my cottage, freeing up the guest cottages for the group that was soon to arrive. We put the finishing touches on the inn, cleaning the outdoor furniture and putting fresh flowers in each of the rooms. That evening the entire staff joined us for dinner.

At midmorning the next day, Myra and Shelby joined us in the bar. We drank coffee while waiting for the new guests to arrive. Normally cool and collected, Adrienne was as jumpy as a long-tailed cat in a room full of rocking chairs. She had already swiped three cigarettes from me and was eyeing the one I was about to light. Shelby helped to keep our minds off things by sharing her dreams for a new medical clinic on the island.

The unmistakable sound of the van crunching up the oyster-shell drive drew all of our attention. Adrienne and I got up and prepared to meet our guests. Their arrival was less chaotic than the last group's. Everyone introduced themselves and migrated into the bar where we served up the drinks. Annie and Liz had arrived drunk, and for the moment, were the life of the party.

The lesbians of the group seemed to band together instantly, leaving William, who preferred to be called Billy, and his lover Chris to mingle with the Burkes. Brandon Fallon chose a table away from the group and studied the place with an odd expression.

I watched Adrienne as she studied him intently, her brow furrowed in concentration. I wondered if anything had popped into her mind. The curiosity was driving me nuts, but I was too close to the other guests to ask discreetly.

Brandon was an average-looking man. I guessed he was in his early forties. He reminded me of the accountant who once prepared my taxes. He had a head full of blonde hair that he kept swept to one side. He was even fairer skinned than I was, and from the looks of him he never ventured out into the sun.

Iris and the staff set out their usual barbecue spread in the bar. "What the hell is this?" Billy asked, holding up a conch fritter. Chris leaned over and whispered in his ear. "I'm not eating that shit!" Billy griped as he dropped the fritter back onto the platter. I agreed wholeheartedly about the conch, but at least I had better manners than to voice it the way he did.

Myra and Shelby exchanged amazed glances at how accurately Adrienne had described Billy and Chris. They watched the other guests intently to see if they were also as she had described. I giggled as each time they looked at each other incredulously.

Billy reminded me of an overgrown Harry Potter, complete with the little glasses. He was a pudgy man with a boyish face. His belly protruded over his belt, making him look like he was expecting a baby in a few days. I got tickled when I looked at his delicate little hands. They were so soft I doubted he had ever seen a hard day's work in his life.

Chris was the same height as Billy but was in much better shape. He kept his thinning brown hair cropped short, unlike his lover, who looked a little shaggy. Chris had a sweet boyish face with bright blue eyes. He looked like the typical kid next door.

Jerri and Richard Burke openly appraised everyone in the bar. In conversation, they of course said that they were looking for someplace different to vacation. They spent most of their meal ogling the women, and I had to resist the urge to slap them both upside the head.

They made an odd-looking couple. Jerri was tall and slender, with short dark hair and dark eyes. Her husband Richard was a redhead with freckles all over his body. He was short with a slightly muscular build. The spider tattoo on the back of his hand looked like he had done it himself while three sheets to the wind.

Brandon hung around the bar after most of the crowd had retired to their cottages. He asked a lot of questions about the inn, strange questions about things most guests would never have cared to know. I began to wonder if he was interested in buying and was considering our place as a prospect.

When we were finally alone in the bar, Myra, Shelby, and I made a beeline for Adrienne. Like the paparazzi, we barraged her with questions to see if she had learned anything new.

She swiped another cigarette from me, and I began to worry that Brandon was going to turn her into a full-time smoker. "I'm sorry to disappoint you, girls, but I still have nothing. I at least get a little something on everyone else, but nothing on him at all."

Myra giggled. "What do you get on me?"

Adrienne laughed. "It doesn't work like that. I can't just read your thoughts when I want to. Your thoughts flow through my head at random. However, I do know that you're excited about being able to live here and write computer programs for your customers back home."

Myra looked astonished. "That's absolutely amazing!"

"Not really. You mentioned it the other night at dinner," Adrienne said with a mischievous grin.

"I suppose it helps to have a sense of humor about it," Shelby said. "I'm sure you learn things that you never wanted to know."

"True. Sometimes it feels like a curse. I don't really understand it myself, this gift. I find it hard to explain it to people, so I rarely tell anyone about it. I learned that lesson the hard way."

Adrienne's words made me feel even worse about my initial reaction to her gift. Especially knowing how she felt about me even then made me feel like a complete ass. I made up my mind at that moment to never chastise her for it, even in jest.

We spent the rest of the afternoon sitting there in the bar, talking and getting to know each other better. I knew Shelby and Myra would eventually have to return to the mainland to make their moving arrangements, and I dreaded the thought. It was wonderful having someone around that we had bonded with so quickly.

At dinner that night, we all paid special attention to Brandon because we wanted to learn more about him—and because we found it hard to make pleasant conversation with Billy and the Burkes. Brandon was quiet, and it was an effort to keep him talking. When it seemed he was becoming annoyed with our prodding, we stopped harassing him.

"What do you suggest we plan for tomorrow?" Madyson asked. She was a little cutie. She looked very young with long blonde hair that she wore in a braid down her back. She was so tiny. I felt like a giant when I stood next to her, and Adrienne completely dwarfed her.

Her girlfriend Emily was just as petite. Her reddish brown hair hung just past her shoulders and accented her hazel eyes. I figured she and Madyson were in their early twenties.

"There are a lot of interesting sights on the island. The porters are native islanders and are very knowledgeable of all the points of interest. If the weather is pretty tomorrow, I suggest a trip to Mt. Alvernia. On a clear day, the view from the mountaintop is breathtaking. We can have Iris and her staff pack lunches for anyone who goes, and you can make an afternoon of it if you wish." Adrienne looked at me with an approving glance after my little speech. I was starting to become comfortable in my role as innkeeper.

"That sounds perfect," Madyson said, and Emily nodded in agreement. To my supreme satisfaction, the Burkes and Billy and Chris liked the idea as well and said that they would enjoy going. The rest of the group opted to spend the day on the beach. Brandon did not express a desire to do either.

After dinner, we went into the bar where the Burkes and Billy and his lover played poker. The lesbians of the group bonded with us quickly, and we all sat together talking and drinking. Brandon sat alone and kept looking down the driveway, as if expecting someone to arrive.

"I invited that Brandon guy to come and sit with us, but he said he'd rather not." Abigail glanced over at him. "I kind of feel sorry for him. Billy was on his case on the flight to the island. He kept asking him all kinds of questions and berating him for no reason. He acted like a schoolyard bully."

"I wonder why he came here alone. He doesn't seem to want to mingle with anyone, just sit there by himself. Doesn't his behavior strike anyone else as odd?" Shelby asked.

I listened and watched as the girls discussed Brandon. It was going to be a little easier committing the current guests' names to memory. I liked Abigail and Sandy. They were closer in age to Adrienne and me, and we shared a lot of the same interests.

Abigail was upbeat and very friendly, with a pretty wicked sense of humor. Sandy was friendly as well, but significantly more reserved than her outgoing partner. She had a unique birthmark on the side of her neck that resembled a little cat paw, which I thought was adorable.

Abigail sighed. "He looks so sad. I wish he would join us. At least he'd have someone to talk to."

"I think he's a little weird, if you ask me." Annie interjected. "I don't like the way he stares at us, and I don't think he's shy, just unsociable."

Annie and Liz had to be in their early twenties. Both of them had multiple body piercings, and I shuddered to think of the other things they might have pierced that we could not readily see. It hurt me just thinking about it. They wore tops that showed off their midriffs and had matching tattoos around their belly buttons.

I remembered Adrienne saying they had only been together six months, which explained why they seemed to be joined at the hip. When one got up to go to the restroom, the other was sure to follow. They stayed in there a little longer every time they went. I figured they were either having sex or doing drugs. Neither would have surprised me. Of course, we all had to talk about them when they were gone.

"What's up with the multicolored hair?" Madyson asked.

"It's the in thing. I'm thinking about getting a pink stripe down the middle of my head, myself," I said, and Madyson stared at me in disbelief before she realized I was kidding.

"You know, I'm only in my mid thirties, but I feel so old next to them. Maybe I should get something pierced. You have any suggestions, Hayden?" Adrienne wiggled her eyebrows at me.

"Get your tongue pierced," Liz said as she and Annie rejoined us at the table.

"I don't think I could handle that. It looks way too painful to me." Adrienne grimaced.

Annie flicked her tongue out at us. "It doesn't hurt all that bad. Have any of you ever had a woman go down on you with a pierced tongue?" I had, but there was no way I was admitting it to the group. Still, there's something to be said for that little steel ball coming in contact with—

"Hayden?" Adrienne disturbed my reminiscing.

"Huh?"

"What do you say? Should I go for it and get my tongued pierced?"

"No, my love. No need to mess with perfection. That tongue of yours has many skills."

"Hey, I have an idea," Abigail said. "This will help us all get to know each other a little better. Everyone at the table has to tell about their first sexual experience with a woman. You have to disclose how old you were and who you were with. Is everybody in?"

We all looked at each other. "Okay, I'm in," Adrienne said and winked at me. My love would do just about anything to please our guests. I rolled my eyes at her, but when Myra agreed to it I knew I was stuck.

"Um, okay, who goes first?" I asked, looking at Shelby.

"Not me! I think since Abigail came up with the idea then she has to go first."

"No problem," Abigail said with a grin. "I was fifteen."

"Wow! I was more interested in basketball at that age. I guess I led a sheltered life," Shelby admitted.

Myra rolled her eyes. "Please continue, Abigail."

"My best friend and I were inseparable. We talked about everything, and one day we got on the topic of sex with another woman. For a while we just talked about it in general. Then we got more specific, like what it would be like between us. One afternoon after school, we decided to give it a try. Her mom wasn't feeling well and came home early from work. I've never moved so fast in my life."

Abigail broke into a fit of laughter. "I put my shirt on inside out. When her mom came into the room, we looked so guilty. She demanded to know what we'd been up to. My best friend Kelly was the best liar in the world. She told her mom that we had been trying on her clothes. I don't know if she really believed us, but it got us off the hook. I didn't try that again until I got into college."

"Oh, I would have just died." Myra laughed. "I would have fainted the minute I heard her mother come into the house."

"All right, since I went first, I get to pick who goes next. I pick Adrienne," Abigail said.

Adrienne cleared her throat. I got tickled at the fact that it made her nervous to be put on the spot. Served her right for agreeing to this stupid game.

"I was seventeen. I had a huge crush on the girl next door. We walked to school together every day, and I had to suffer through listening to her talk about all the cute boys she had classes with. We were both seniors, and for senior skip day, we went to a guy's house for a pool party. Needless to say, we got totally smashed. She and I went into the bathhouse to change out of our swimsuits. I remember I was so afraid to take my clothes off in front of her, so I wrapped myself up in a towel and tugged my wet suit off under it."

I watched Adrienne in amusement. Her face had turned completely red, and she nervously tucked her hair behind her ear. She stared off into space as she talked, reliving the events as she told them.

"When I had finally gotten undressed—this took a little while because I was clutching the towel so tight around me—she grabbed it and ripped it off me. There I stood, completely naked in front of the girl I secretly drooled over. And all I could do was just stand there with my mouth hanging open. The next thing I know, she leaned in and kissed me. I lost my virginity on the floor of the bathhouse in some kid's backyard. Then I went home and threw up jungle juice for the next two days, and that was it."

"Wait, didn't you two do anything after that?" Madyson asked.

"Nope. She lost interest in me after that and pursued someone else. It was my first time, and I'm sure I wasn't that impressive. I was heartbroken for a while, but I eventually got over it."

"Aw, Adrienne, that's kind of sad." Myra reached across the table and patted her on the arm.

"Yeah, well, I didn't miss out on much. Seems she was a little on the loose side. She dated her way through the football team and got pregnant before graduation." Adrienne laughed. "Now I get to pick, and I pick Shelby."

"Ah, you would, you little fart." Shelby grimaced. "Well, I was in my first year of college. I shared a dorm room with the cutest girl. She was young and innocent, or so I thought. We started going places together and just hanging out. We had a lot in common. I had really gotten attached to her, but I had no idea how she felt about me. One night we were bored and drove around town looking for something to do. We ended up just sitting in the car out by the lakes at school and talking.

"This innocent little thing looks over at me and asks out of the blue, 'Shelby, when are you going to kiss me?' I nearly swallowed my tongue. That first kiss landed us in the backseat of my car. I still have the car to this day; I just couldn't part with it. Every anniversary, Myra and I take it back to that same spot on the lake."

"You're kidding me! Myra was your first?"

Myra grinned from ear to ear. "Yep, she was my first. Now you all know my story. So, shall I pick the next victim?"

I knew from the gleam in Myra's eye that she intended to pick me. If she did, I would have to choke her.

"I pick Madyson." My sigh of relief was audible.

"Aw shit!" Madyson exclaimed in embarrassment, her face turning crimson. She immediately began to chew her thumbnail, and her better half grabbed her hand.

"That's disgusting, baby." Emily laughed. "Now spill the beans."

"Shit! All right! Um, I had a big crush on my gym teacher in high school. Everybody knew she was gay, and they always made terrible comments behind her back. I never told a soul I had the hots for her. After I graduated, I started working at a grocery store and my old gym teacher came in there every week. She always came to my register, and we made casual chitchat."

Madyson grabbed the rum from the middle of the table and filled her glass, which she quickly emptied before continuing. "Anyway, one night she came in kind of late. I had just finished my shift and was about to walk back to my apartment. She offered me a ride. I was so nervous my knees knocked the whole two blocks. In the interest of being polite, I asked her if she wanted to come in. And she accepted."

"Yeah, right," we all chimed in, ribbing her mercilessly. She refused to finish the story after that, but another glass of rum loosened her tongue again.

"Well, we talked for a while and had a few glasses of wine. One thing led to another, and we ended up in bed together. In the heat of the moment I made the fatal mistake of screaming out, 'Oh, Miss Stafford!' That's what I had always called her in gym class, and it just came out. Needless to say, that was a real mood killer for her."

I laughed so hard I couldn't catch my breath, imagining the look on Miss Stafford's face. Then I discovered that paybacks truly are a bitch: Madyson picked me to go next.

"My first experience was in high school with the principal's daughter. We went to a party, got smashed, and did it on the bathroom floor. End of story."

My brief and to-the-point story resulted in me being chastised by the entire group. They demanded details, and I was forced to elaborate. "I remember making the first move, but I was too nervous to kiss her right off the bat. I walked up behind her and kissed the back of her neck. My hands were shaking so much I barely got her pants unzipped. I think I had her completely naked before I ever worked up the nerve to actually kiss her. Now, you freaks, that's all I'm telling!"

Adrienne chose that moment to jump in. "According to Gloria, when you got back home you were so drunk you barely knew your own name. In addition, you were proudly wearing a pair of panties around your neck. Oh, and the best part was, you had to wear turtleneck sweaters for nearly two weeks to hide all of the love bites on your neck."

"That's so funny! Shelby and I had no idea what we were doing. It felt great, ya know, but I think we were together a year before either of us had an orgasm. I was like wow, what was that?" Myra said, laughing.

"Myra! They don't need to know that!" Shelby chided, which made it all the funnier.

"Well, it's true! I mean really, when you're that young, you're just fumbling around. I don't know how guys ever figure it out! At least we know what feels good."

"Myra! Have mercy!" Shelby clamped her hand over her mate's mouth to shut her up.

"I know what you mean!" Annie spoke up. "The first time I brought home toys, Liz totally freaked out."

"Bloody hell, woman, shut up." Liz buried her face in her hands.

"Admit it, Liz, you liked them once you got over the initial shock." Myra laughed.

Liz giggled. "I did. After that, I couldn't look at kitchen appliances the same way. I even looked at the egg beater and thought, hmm?"

I was slap-assed drunk and laughing like a fool. Abigail was right, we had gotten to know one another much better. At times, a little too well. We didn't even notice when the rest of the guests turned in for the night.

"Okay, what is the most embarrassing thing that has happened to you during sex?" Abigail asked, keeping the game going.

"I think you all know mine," Madyson said, her face still red.

Shelby piped up. "One time I farted. We weren't doing anything but kissing, though."

"Oh shit, Shelby," Adrienne laughed. "That's gross!"

"Tell me about it! We had Mexican that night," Myra said, with tears of laughter streaming down her face.

"Okay, enough of this. I'm going to be hurting in the morning." Shelby rubbed her glass against her forehead. "Do you realize we've killed four whole bottles of rum?"

We all decided to call it a night. Shelby and Myra were kind enough to help Adrienne and me straighten up the bar, and then we went our separate ways. I giggled all the way back to our cottage.

"You seem to be adapting well to entertaining the guests," Adrienne said as I leaned heavily on her while she opened the door.

"It's not as bad as I thought it was going to be," I admitted. "We have to stop drinking with them, though. If we keep this up, we'll both have to be rehabilitated."

We both fell onto the bed and lay there for a while, hoping the room would stop spinning.

"Hayden, I can't go to sleep like this. I'm gonna be sick if I do. Let's grab some towels and go down to the beach and take a swim."

"Are you nuts? I may pass out and float out to sea." She tugged on my hand until I stood up with her. "I can see two of you, Adrienne, and you both look good." I clumsily grabbed her around the waist.

"Come on, a swim will help clear our heads a little. Besides, you might get lucky." She wiggled her eyebrows. Naturally, I followed her down to the beach like a drooling dog. We stripped off our clothes and walked into the water.

"Damn! This is cold," I said.

"There's only one way to get used to it," Adrienne said and shoved me under the water. The shock of the cold water helped clear my head a little, but I had to retaliate. I sprang out of the water like a cat and returned the favor by pulling her under with me.

The horseplay led to other things and we made love right there in the wet sand before I remembered why it wasn't a good idea to have sex on the beach. I had sand in places I didn't even know I had, and none of them were places where sand ought to be. She exhausted me, and the climb back up the bluff nearly killed us both. I celebrated making it to the top by tossing my cookies next to a banana tree. For me, the party was over.

Robin Alexander

CHAPTER NINE

The next morning, I felt like I had been run over by a truck. I actually prayed that I would be just to end my misery, and it was small comfort to my pounding head and churning stomach that I looked like I already had been at least side-swiped.

Iris was kind enough to send us some tea and toast, which we ate in bed. Neither of us had the strength to move.

"Let's make a pact right here and now that we will never get that drunk again."

Adrienne moaned in agreement as she sipped her tea. After we had food in our stomachs, we took something for the pain. I took a long shower standing on what I thought was a sandbar, then went out to get the guests on their way for the day as Adrienne took her shower.

After everyone had eaten breakfast, I ushered those going on the Mt. Alvernia trip into the van along with the ice chests containing their picnic lunches. I was shocked to see two of the couples that had spent most of the night with us loading up for the trip. I grumbled to myself that I must be getting old as I watched them go about their business bright eyed and bushy tailed.

I thought it strange that Brandon was nowhere in sight, but I was still feeling too puny to ponder it any further. I made a mental note to check on him later and set about my chores for the day.

During the hottest part of the day Iris, Shelby, and Myra joined Adrienne and me in the bar, where we lay around on the chaise lounges. "Has anyone seen Brandon today?" I wondered out loud.

"My head still hurts too bad to notice anything," Myra groaned, "but no, I haven't seen him."

"Maybe he struck out on his own this morning. He does seem to be sort of a loner," Shelby said thoughtfully.

I figured he'd done just that. I had a gnawing feeling in my gut, though; something about that man troubled me. It made no sense to me why a single man would come here alone. The other thing that bothered me was Brandon didn't seem to be gay. He seemed to take an interest in the women and stared at them with what I considered a lustful gaze. When I found him looking at Adrienne that way, it had made my hackles rise.

Brandon wasn't at dinner that night either, and my curiosity turned to worry. I asked Iris and found that there had been no answer when she'd sent someone over that morning to ask if he wanted breakfast. I went to his cottage and knocked on the door. Receiving no answer, I gingerly tried the door and was alarmed when it opened. I called his name a few times before venturing in. His bed had obviously not been slept in.

I walked farther into the room and noticed his suitcase had not been unpacked. Quick inspection of the bathroom revealed that he had not been in there either. His entire cottage was seemingly untouched.

I met Adrienne back in the bar. She looked at me questioningly, and I shook my head. I watched as her brow furrowed in worry. Neither of us wanted to discuss the matter in front of the other guests, though no one else seemed to notice that one of the group was missing.

Fortunately, our guests turned in earlier than they had the previous night, giving Adrienne and me a chance to talk and enjoy a drink. I poured us a couple of iced teas, not wanting a replay of the previous night, and joined her at the table. She had made herself welcome to my cigarettes and was nervously puffing away when I sat down.

"What's troubling you, baby?"

"Brandon will not be back, Hayden." She exhaled the smoke and took a large gulp of her drink. I noticed how her hands shook as she lifted the cigarette to her lips.

"What do you mean, he won't be back?"

"He's dead," she said flatly.

It took a minute for her words to sink in. I sat dumbfounded.

"Hayden, Hank killed him. When I woke up I could hear his thoughts pounding through my head. He was so angry, and he was relieved when he took Brandon's life. I don't have any idea what he did with the body, but I do know that he beat him to death." Adrienne shuddered.

"Why haven't you told me this before now?" I asked, still dazed.

"I had hoped that I was wrong, but when you confirmed that he never slept in his room, I knew for sure."

"Why on earth would he do such a thing?" I asked before taking a huge gulp of my drink.

Adrienne pressed her glass to her temple. "I think he knew Brandon. Hank was furious, and it occurred to him that he would have to kill Brandon. I believe Brandon knew something about Hank that caused Hank to murder him."

"We have to call the police, Adrienne."

"What exactly do I tell them? If they don't think I did it, then they'll assume I've gone crazy!"

"Well, we can't let a murderer roam loose among us." I was trying my best not to push Adrienne's buttons, but I was having a hard time keeping my cool. My agitation was being fueled by my fear, and I was finding it hard to be supportive.

"Hayden, we don't have a police station on the island. There is one member of the Bahamian police who resides here; however, I'm reluctant to confide in him until we find a body."

"When you say we, what exactly does that mean?" I was so hoping she was not going to say that we had to go in search of a corpse.

"To get Colie to do a formal inquiry, we need to be able to produce a body." She opened a fresh pack of cigarettes.

"What if we go to—who is Colie?"

"Colie is the policeman who lives on the island."

"Okay, how about we go to Colie and tell him that we have a guest who is missing from the inn. Perhaps he'll find Brandon's body, and then he'll call for help with the investigation."

Adrienne smiled for the first time all day. "That's a great idea. I'll call him first thing in the morning. No sense in calling him out here in the middle of the night. I'm sure he wouldn't appreciate it and would chalk it up to a single man just out having a good time."

Neither of us slept well at all that night. I went through the motion of locking our cottage door, but a child could get through that flimsy lock if he had a mind to. When Saber made it known that he wanted to go out by slapping the bedside clock off the table, it nearly sent us both into the ceiling fan.

"Why doesn't he just meow like a normal cat?" Adrienne exclaimed, holding her hand over her heart.

"I'm not sure, but if he does that again, I'm going to kill him with my bare hands. After I get out of the cardiac care unit, that is," I groused, crawling back into bed.

When the sun cast its first rays across the eastern sky, we both climbed out of bed feeling more exhausted than when we'd first lain down. I passed on breakfast that morning and assisted the porters in loading the van for the day's excursion. Most of the group were anxious to see the sights, but Annie and Liz had chosen to remain behind and sun on the beach again.

I felt a bit guilty hoping that Billy might get a visit from ol' mister snake. I didn't feel guilty about wanting that for Billy, but about hurting the snake. I pitied anything that had to put its mouth on him, especially Billy's lover Chris.

After they finished breakfast, I went into drill sergeant mode. I had them in that van before they knew what hit them. I did, however, toss a bottle of bug repellent in, feeling a little bad about snatching the biscuit out of Billy's mouth and shoving him into the waiting vehicle.

"Okay, let's call Colie," I said as I ran into the bar, not realizing that Shelby and Myra had joined Adrienne there. Both of them turned, looking at me questioningly.

"Adrienne, please call Colie while I bring the ladies up to speed." I could see the relief on Adrienne's face when she realized she wouldn't have to be the one to tell them about Hank and Brandon.

By the time she completed the call, I had explained what we knew so far. Shelby and Myra both sat in stunned silence. Adrienne joined us at the table and immediately lit up a cigarette.

"What did he say?" I asked as I lit my own.

"He'll be right over. His sister is going to start calling the other inns just in case," Adrienne said, deliberately not looking at the speechless women sitting next to me.

Finally, Shelby asked, "I'm sorry if I sound like an ass asking this, but did you know anything about this man before you hired him as your handyman?"

"Gloria hired him before I came here. I don't know what she knew of him. Aside from his looks, I thought he was all right if Gloria felt comfortable with him."

A thought occurred to me. "Look, I know this has got to be alarming to you both. Please don't feel like you have to stay here if you're afraid for your safety."

Myra was the first to speak, and Shelby nodded emphatically at her words. "We are not leaving you two to deal with this situation alone. You've taken us in like family, and we plan to stick by your side. Your offer is very considerate, but we're here for the duration."

I was truly moved. It was apparent to both Adrienne and me that they were resolved to stay. It was comforting, to say the least, but I was still worried about their safety.

True to his word, Colie arrived shortly after Adrienne made the call. He was at the very least six foot five inches. His skin was darker than Iris's, which I hadn't thought possible. Judging from the size of his arms and chest, he spent many hours building up his body. He was a very imposing figure, and I doubted that anyone had ever been foolish enough to test his patience.

However, when he spoke he was extremely genteel. He politely accepted a cup of coffee from Iris and rewarded her with a warm smile that did not go unnoticed by the occupants of the table. Had I not been so stressed by the recent events, I might have been tempted to play Cupid.

Adrienne drew his attention back to the table. "Colie, please allow me to introduce you to everyone." She motioned to me first. "This is my partner, Hayden, and this is Shelby and Myra." He shook our hands with a firm grip, but when introduced to Iris, he simply smiled. If I didn't know better I would have sworn that the giant of a man was a little smitten with her.

He took out a notepad and a little stubby pencil and prepared to take down information. We gave an account of what we knew about Brandon as Colie scribbled and asked a few questions.

Although I didn't think that Colie's career had seen much serious investigative work on a sparsely populated island that seemed to need nothing more than a one-man police force, I was quite impressed by his initiative. Had we been in the States, we would still probably be waiting in a line just to file a missing persons report. Yet, Colie had already organized a search party that was combing the island as we spoke.

He assured us before departing that he would contact us the minute he had any news. All of us felt reassured by his diligence and breathed a sigh of relief. We tried to keep our minds off things by playing a couple of games of poker. I threw in the towel when Iris relieved me of the last of my cash. Our dear Iris was a true card shark.

Adrienne was giving Iris a run for her money and stayed in the game, so I decided to go for a walk and stretch my legs. The breeze was starting to pick up and made for a pleasant venture down the path that led to the beach. The plants that we had set out along the bluff seemed to be flourishing in their new home. I spent a little time there looking over our handiwork before heading down to the beach.

My eyes nearly bugged out of my head when I began to descend the staircase. Annie and Liz were spread out on the sand, naked as the day they were born. From my vantage point, my suspicions were confirmed: they had all of their parts pierced and adorned with jewelry. I winced inwardly, thinking how much it must have hurt to have some of those places jammed through with a steel post. I admired the scenery for a moment and decided it would probably be a better idea to walk elsewhere.

As I turned to make my way back up the path, an amused pair of eyes met mine. "What are you looking at, Hayden?" Adrienne asked, cocking one eyebrow.

I pointed to the beach. "I was looking at those two naked women down there." No sense in hiding it, I was cold busted.

"Hayden! You're a little pervert, aren't you?"

"I'll show you a pervert," I said as I chased her back to our cottage. For the rest of the afternoon, I showed her every little perversion I could pull out of my bag of tricks.

At dinner that night, the very question I had hoped to avoid popped up. Jerri Burke asked around a mouthful of food, "Where is that guy who came here by himself? I haven't seen him since the night we got here."

I cleared my throat. "We don't know where Brandon is. We became concerned when he didn't show for breakfast this morning, and we called the local police. There is the possibility that he met someone from another inn or hotel on the island. He may have decided to spend time with someone away from here and just didn't tell anyone he'd be away, so the police are checking it all out." I hoped I sounded convincing as the half-truths slid out.

"He's probably off getting a piece of ass," Billy said smugly. "A man does have his needs. Unlike women, that's just something we have to have."

"Thank you for clearing that up for us, Harry—I mean Billy. We tend to forget that men are such sexual predators since we have nothing to do with them. You know, being lesbians and all." I returned his smug expression.

Shelby quickly jumped in and changed the subject before I had a chance to really tag the pudgy bastard. I suppose I should have been grateful. It would have been bad for business had I crawled across the table and pummeled him with my dinner plate, which, by the way, had a cleverly hidden piece of conch in the salad, adding to my ire.

After dinner, as was our custom, we all filed into the bar. Billy, Chris, and the Burkes settled down to their nightly game of cards while the rest of the gang sat at the bar to drink and chat. I was surprised to see Colie arrive, and my heart sank when I noticed his grim expression.

"Is there somewhere we can talk privately?" he asked, pulling me aside.

I gestured for Adrienne to follow. Myra and Shelby immediately took over, serving drinks and entertaining the guests. I owed them big-time.

We went back to the cottage that Adrienne and I shared and sat at the table so we could enjoy the breeze.

"I'm sorry to bring you bad news," Colie said as he sat. "We found Brandon's wallet near Bad Hole. There was also blood on the ground. It looks as though he may have been dragged through the brush and dumped there, although we did not find any trace of his body.

"I don't want to scare either of you, but my hunch is that someone killed him and dumped his body in the hole. As I am sure you already know, the locals avoid Bad Hole like the plague. If I were going to commit a murder on this island, I can't think of a better place to dispose of a body."

Cold chills ran down my spine. I no longer doubted Adrienne's abilities, but to have it confirmed in such a manner brought reality home. I reached under the table and took her hand in mine. I had no idea how she would react to hearing the news. I could feel her hand trembling as I held it.

Colie continued, "I have called in the authorities from Nassau to do a more thorough investigation. They are also arranging for a dive team to come in and search for his remains. My sister has placed a few calls to the States to see if she can locate his family. In addition, the Bahamian police are working with the authorities in the States to see what they can find regarding his background. That's all we have for now, I'm afraid."

"Colie, do you have any idea who would do such a thing?" I asked.

"We have no leads yet. I'll probably have to question the guests and staff, depending on our findings. Until then, I would like to keep a lid on all of this."

"We understand," I said, speaking for Adrienne as well.

Shelby and Myra were beside themselves until the guests retired for the night. We sat at one of the tables in the bar with a bottle of spiced rum and four glasses, and I relayed what we had learned. Myra became visibly pale, and I assumed she felt as I did hearing what Adrienne had said eerily confirmed.

"How do we lead them to Hank?" Shelby asked.

"Colie said that depending on what they found out, he might need to interview the guests and staff. Hopefully, by Hank's appearance alone they'll suspect him and dig a little deeper. I suppose we just have to wait and see," Adrienne said.

"Do we even know if Hank is still on the island? What if he already left?" Myra asked.

"He's still here," Adrienne confirmed. "He's looking for something and is very upset that he can't find it. Leaving the island is not an option until he recovers what he has lost."

"I take it you still don't know what it is," I said while Adrienne stole the cigarette that I had just lit.

"No, but I do know that it's buried somewhere on the grounds of the inn. Maybe we could do a little digging on our own. If we find what he's searching for and hide it again, then he will be forced to stay on the island. The longer he stays, the better the chances that Colie will find evidence to incriminate him."

Shelby shook her head. "Won't he think it strange that we're digging too? He may realize that we're on to him then and decide to do something rash. I say let him get his shit and go. Whatever it is, it was worth killing a man for, and frankly I don't want to find it."

"Shelby, we can't just let a cold-blooded murderer go free," Myra said as she rubbed the tension from Shelby's shoulders. "We have to dig around in a way that won't look suspicious to him."

A grin made its way across my face. I had a plan. "When we were clearing the land behind the cottages, I noticed that there were all sorts of tropical plants growing wild around here. We can dig them up and replant them on our property. That will give us an excuse to dig around. If we find nothing, it's no loss because we'll have improved the landscaping around the inn."

Even Shelby agreed that the plan was a good one, though she maintained her reservations about our safety, and we decided that the next morning we would sketch out a couple of designs for our new landscaping project. Everyone agreed that we would have to start off slow because of the guests.

I was afraid we would find what Hank had been feverishly searching for, which made this a very dangerous venture. With any luck, though, I still hoped we would dig up something we could use to prove Hank had a motive for murder.

CHAPTER TEN

S helby, make sure you get as much dirt around the roots as possible," I grunted as I lifted the palm into the wheelbarrow. "We may have to come back out here and dig up some more dirt to make the beds. There's so much sand in the soil on the island. This little thicket is the first place I've actually found something resembling dirt."

"Don't worry, Monkey Chops, I got it under control. This is not the first time I've dug up a plant or two. You wouldn't believe the honey-do lists Myra has for me around the house. Sometimes I have to go back to work just to get some rest. Don't let that feminine façade of hers fool you; she's every bit as strong as I am. I think she just likes to bark orders."

I took a break and sat on the edge of the wheelbarrow. "Shelby, I'm worried about Adrienne. I know Hank doesn't know anything about her gift, but I can't help but feel the more she learns, the more danger she'll be in. I can't stand the thought of him roaming loose like this. He beat that man to death, according to Adrienne, with the intent of killing him. If he had an inkling that Adrienne possessed the power that she does, nothing would stop him from coming for her."

Shelby grimaced as she spoke. "That's why I was so opposed to this digging idea. What if he sees us doing it and feels threatened? We already know what he does when he gets desperate."

"I know this is a stupid idea. It's going to be like looking for a needle in a haystack, but I just can't sit by and do nothing. We're in a no-win situation. We're stuck with him until he finds what he's looking for. I have a lot of respect for Colie, but we can't put him on Hank's path without exposing Adrienne. I'm at a loss here." I could feel the fear and frustration welling up in my throat, but there was no way I was going to lose it in front of anyone, let alone Shelby.

"I know, Monkey Chops. All I'm saying is we have to be very careful. In addition to digging around the inn, I think we need to keep tabs on Hank. I'd feel better knowing where he was at all times. Isn't there some sort of project we can assign him to?"

"You're right, it's a good idea to have him do something so we can keep an eye on him." After a second or two, I broke out in a grin. "What can we break that would keep him busy for a while?"

"Let me ponder that while we head back to the inn." Shelby grabbed the wheelbarrow handles. "Now get your magnolia ass up, Miss Daisy. I ain't hauling you and these plants too."

Sitting in the cool of the bar, Shelby and I discussed our idea with Adrienne and Myra. We brainstormed for a while until Myra hit upon the idea of flushing tampons down the commodes to stop up the sewer. Disgusting as it was, it was the only plan we could come up with. That afternoon, we put Operation Massive Flush into action.

Adrienne and I giggled as we flushed almost an entire box of tampons. We were beginning to worry that it wouldn't work when the toilet finally backed up. To add the icing on the cake, Billy sent Chris to inform us that he was having problems with his toilet too. I could just imagine that big goof sitting on the toilet with the funnies. It was enough to keep me from joining them for dinner that night.

Adrienne and I made the trek over to Hank's place, which could only be described as a shack. I expected no less from the pirate. He met us as the door with his usual piggish grunt.

"Hi, Hank," Adrienne said, trying to sound casual. "We have a major problem at the inn. It seems the sewer is backing up again, and with the place full of guests we need some help quick."

After a string of curses that burned even my ears, Hank assured us that he would be along shortly. I toyed with the idea of taking a self-guided tour of his mansion while he worked on the sewer but thought better of it, remembering what he looked like with that monkey wrench. Hopefully, that would be something that Colie and his team would undertake.

When we arrived back at the inn, Iris informed us that Colie was waiting for us at Adrienne's cottage. We found him sitting at the table out front dining on a full plate of fried chicken with all the trimmings. It was obvious that Iris believed in the old adage that the quickest way to a man's heart was through his stomach.

"Good evening, ladies," Colie greeted us warmly with a face covered in chicken debris. "I have some more news for you. We'll be working with the DEA on this one. Mr. Fallon had ties to a drug cartel that has been very active in the Bahamian islands as well as the States. We believe his death was associated with drug runners."

Adrienne and I exchanged glances. I was concerned that they would start looking in the wrong direction, which prompted my next move. I looked at Adrienne a moment, pleading with my eyes. When she looked confused, I tried to think of a crafty way to throw some suspicion in Hank's direction.

"Colie, I've noticed something strange going on, and I hope you will humor my paranoia and look into it."

Colie set his chicken down and wiped his hands. He took out his notepad, and he and Adrienne looked at me expectantly.

"We have a handyman working for us named Hank." I felt Adrienne's body stiffen as I spoke. She grabbed my knee with a grip so tight that I almost second-guessed bringing it up.

"He's been acting real strange. Not that he's not strange to begin with, but he's acting even stranger since all of this began.

Maybe it's just me, but I think it's worth looking into." I patted Adrienne's hand under the table in an attempt to calm her and bring circulation back to my leg.

"How so?" Colie's brow furrowed as he waited for me to continue.

"He's been digging all around the grounds of the inn. I became suspicious when he broke our sewer line. He said it was leaking and he just dug it up to fix it. But the hole he dug was big enough to bury an army in. When we cleared the land behind the cottages we found evidence of digging there also. I just find it very odd."

Colie sat silent for a moment. He looked at us both thoughtfully. "How would his digging be related to Brandon's murder?"

I truly realized Adrienne's dilemma at that moment. If I didn't tell him all that I knew, the digging would seem unrelated.

"Maybe it's not, Colie, but don't you think it's odd that a man who looks just like a pirate suddenly has the urge to dig up the grounds all around the inn?" It sounded ludicrous to me as it rolled out of my mouth.

"I don't think Hank is connected to this, but I'll run a background check on him just to be on the safe side. As I said before, we believe Brandon had ties to a drug cartel. I think he may have crossed the wrong person in his organization and came here to hide out. By no means is the investigation closed. We will continue to pursue what leads we have. I promise you both we'll keep you informed.

"Also, we'd like to interview all of your guests. According to their background checks, there's nothing to tie any of them to Brandon Fallon. However, we intend to investigate everyone who has had anything to do with Brandon since his arrival, and since Hank is a member of your staff we'll question him as well. Have you told the guests anything about the investigation?"

Adrienne spoke for the first time. "Not much, but they have noticed that Brandon is missing and some of them have questioned us as to his whereabouts. We told them that he was missing and that you were searching the other inns. They assumed he found someone to play with."

"Good. Let's keep a lid on this until we come to question them. No need to upset anyone with the gory details."

When Colie left, Adrienne abruptly got up and went into her cottage. The slamming of the door was a sure indication that I had screwed up royally. Saber was kind enough to join me at the table and curled up in my lap. I smoked a cigarette and stroked the cat lovingly, giving Adrienne a little while to cool down.

"Well, cat man, it's time for me to take my beating," I said a few minutes later as I got up and made my way to the door. When I walked into the room I was relieved to find no objects being hurled at me. I walked meekly into the bathroom where Adrienne reclined, soaking in the bath.

I put the seat down on the gurgling toilet and sat. A pair of beautiful eyes focused on me, and I shuddered at the anger I saw there.

"What in the hell did you think you were doing, Hayden?"

"Adrienne, I was afraid they were going to go off on a wild goose chase. I was trying to get Colie to focus on Hank."

"Just once, trust my instincts on this. I've lived with this thingy, as you like to call it, all of my life. You can't just give someone a tidbit of info and hope they will see the big picture. I have no desire for the entire island to learn any more than they may have already surmised of my freakish little talent."

"Baby, you are not a freak. I would never expose your ability, that's not my place. I'm just worried about having a psycho pirate running around killing people while the police look in the opposite direction. Nevertheless, I was wrong. I should have discussed it with you before I opened my mouth to Colie."

She looked at me for a long time. When I didn't see forgiveness, I made my best attempt at puppy-dog eyes. Receiving no favorable response, I whipped out the big gun. I flashed a tit. Okay, so it was a little gun, but it got a giggle out of her.

"Hayden, we have to find what Hank is looking for before he does. That's the only way we'll be able to convince Colie to look closer at him. We have to find a way to keep him busy so we can search for whatever it is he lost."

With that in mind, I went to check on the plumber pirate. I found him at the cleanout, snaking the drain. A never-ending string of obscenities spewed out of his mouth while he worked. I was glad when he turned down my offer to assist. I snickered all the way to the bar.

Upon entering the bar, I found Billy holding court and complaining about the problems the inn was having with the sewer system. I apologized to the guests, who all seemed to understand, with the exception of Billy, of course. In an attempt to rid us of Harry Potter, I offered to put up anyone who wanted to go to another inn. Surprisingly, everyone insisted on staying, saying the plumbing was only a minor inconvenience. Surprisingly, Billy shut up then.

Since Sarah had the bar under control, I decided to spend a little time with Myra and Shelby. We sat at one of the tables apart from the rest of the gang. None of them seemed to pay us any mind, which made me happy. I wasn't in the mood to field any questions regarding the disappearance of Brandon Fallon.

Billy and Chris were playing cards with Sandy and Abigail. The customary calypso music on the sound system had been swapped out, and Madyson and Emily moved into the middle of the floor when a slow song began to play. I was surprised to see Annie and Jerri go to the floor as well, leaving Jerri's husband to talk to Liz.

Adrienne had told me that it wasn't uncommon for an occasional straight couple to come to the inn, but the Burkes had made their agenda blatantly obvious. For the most part, all the other couples seemed to avoid them, but tonight Annie and Liz looked to be enjoying their company.

For the first time since all of this messy business with Hank began, my attention was transfixed on something else.

We all watched as Jerri and Annie danced. Jerri ran her fingertips up and down Annie's back. Annie seemed to enjoy her attentions, and Liz watched her lover in someone else's arms with an amused expression.

I glanced over at Shelby and Myra, who were taking in the display. "Surely Annie and Liz are not going to entertain those two?" I said, filling my glass with spiced rum.

"Looks like it, Monkey Chops. They've been as thick as thieves all night. To each his own, I guess." Shelby swiped the bottle from me and filled her own glass.

"How can Liz just sit there and let Jerri paw at Annie like that? I would lose my mind, and the ass whuppings would commence," Myra said in disgust as she stole Shelby's glass of rum.

"Hey, Hayden. Did you ever find that goofy-ass Brandon?" Billy yelled from across the bar.

"We assume he went off in search of a piece of ass, as you so eloquently put it," Adrienne answered as she strolled into the bar, effectively silencing the boisterous man as Chris looked on in embarrassment.

When she joined us at the table she said, "Hank is finished with the sewer line. He was cursing loudly at the pile of tampons he pulled out of the drain. We have to break something else that will be more time consuming."

We all groaned, trying to think of something to keep Hank occupied.

"I think someone should take a look around his house while the rest of us keep him occupied," Myra interjected.

Shelby shook her head vehemently. "No way! What if he catches us?"

"We'll just have to make sure that doesn't happen. It's worth a try. Maybe it will speed things up. Shelby, we are not leaving this island until that man is behind bars," Myra said with conviction.

To my surprise, Adrienne agreed with Myra. "I think we should give it a try. We need to think of another project for him to work on while two of us sneak over to his place. I think we should do it tomorrow."

"Look!" Myra said in a hushed tone. We watched as Jerri and Richard left with Liz and Annie. "I don't even want to think about what those four are going off to do." She stole another full glass of rum from Shelby.

The four of us exchanged glances with Billy and Chris. I shrugged my shoulders, but Billy sneered at me and taunted, "I suppose some women are just as bad as us men."

"Some women, but not this woman," I said, staring him down.

When all of the guests retired from the bar, we quickly cleaned up. Exhausted from stress, Adrienne and I passed on Myra and Shelly's offer for another drink. We made a beeline for our cottage and were asleep in no time.

In the middle of the night, Adrienne shook me awake. "Hayden, get up! Now, baby! There's a snake in Madyson and Emily's cottage!"

"That thingy works in your sleep?" I asked, pulling on a pair of shorts.

"No, I heard them screaming 'snake.' Hurry!"

I grabbed a very sleepy Saber from the bed and tucked him under my arm as I ran toward their cottage. He protested loudly as I made my way down the trail. I could feel the hair rising all down my spine at the thought of what we might find in their room.

The cottage door was wide open. I almost snickered at the two completely naked women standing on top of the bed and pointing at the floor.

"It's under the bed!" Madyson yelled as she shuddered in what appeared to be fear mixed with disgust.

"How big is it?" I asked, still holding Saber tightly in my arms.

"Not very big, only about two feet long, but it's still freaking me out," Emily said. Belatedly remembering her nakedness, she pulled the sheet up, trying to cover herself and Madyson.

Saber, sensing or smelling the snake, struggled in my arms to be let down. I set him down on the floor, and a low growl rumbled out of his chest. He went straight to the bed and peered under, and then shot off like a rocket. There were no sounds except his paws scratching the stone floor. A minute later he emerged from under the bed with the dead grass snake dangling from his mouth, growling loudly to let us know this was his kill. He strolled out of the cottage triumphantly into the night.

Madyson sank down to the bed. "How the hell did that thing get in here?"

Adrienne stared upward thoughtfully before speaking. I followed her gaze, as did Madyson and Emily.

"Surely you don't think it came from the roof?" Emily asked with a shudder.

"I seriously doubt it," Adrienne said in a comforting tone. "We have never had a snake in any of the cottages before. How long has your door been open?"

Emily and Madyson exchanged glances. "We opened it about an hour ago. We, um, we kind of got a little hot and opened it to let the breeze blow through," Madyson answered sheepishly.

"I don't think the snake came in through the roof. I think it came in through the open door. It would be a good idea to keep the door closed, at least during the night," Adrienne advised, and we left them to their business.

When we arrived back at our place I studied the thatched roof intently. "Adrienne, could there be a snake in our roof?"

"I suppose there could be." She crawled sleepily back into our bed. Just as she was getting comfortable, I yanked the covers completely off the bed. She propped herself up on her elbows and stared at me with an arched brow. "Feel better?"

I noted the sarcasm in her tone.

"No, I do not! Why in the hell do we have thatched roofs anyway? They can't hold up all that well in a storm." I tucked the sheet and blanket tightly around the bed after making sure they didn't harbor any snakes.

"They add to the tropical appeal of the inn, and they're treated to repel the rain. We've had very few problems, so don't get any ideas about ripping the roof out of this place, Hayden. Now come to bed or I'm putting you outside with the cat."

I climbed into bed and snuggled as close to Adrienne as I could get. When I heard her breathing become steady, I realized she was almost asleep. I had the creeps, and if I couldn't sleep she wasn't going to either.

"Adrienne?" I whispered into the darkness.

"Hmm," she answered, obviously annoyed.

"Why do you suppose Shelby calls me Monkey Chops? Do I have a monkey face?"

"No, you do not have a monkey face. Now go to sleep."

"You think the snakebite is going to leave a scar?"

The lamp next to the bed clicked on and flooded the room with light. A pair of green eyes narrowed and glared down at me. I gave my best innocent look.

"Hayden, I love you, but if you don't go to sleep I will have to kill you with my bare hands."

I sat straight up. "You love me? Is that any way to tell me for the first time?"

"Honestly, honey, my love for you is the only thing keeping me from choking the life out of you at the moment." She lay back down.

I sat there staring incredulously at her. "Are you serious? Not about the choking part, about the loving me part."

She switched off the light and pulled me down into her arms. I laid my head on her chest and listened to her rapidly beating heart. "Yes, Hayden, I am hopelessly in love with you."

I could tell by her heartbeat she was nervous about admitting her feelings. Then I responded as honestly as I could. "I love you too, Adrienne." I ran the ends of her hair through my fingers and drifted off to sleep.

The next morning we woke up in a mass of tangled arms and legs. I had always hated being held by anyone when I slept, but in Adrienne's case I happily made an exception. When she realized I was awake, she untangled herself from me and looked me in the eyes.

"Did you mean what you said last night?"

Even when she had only just woken up and her hair was a mess, she was the loveliest woman I had ever had the pleasure of being with. "Yes, I meant it. I do love you, Adrienne."

CHAPTER ELEVEN

We sat there all through breakfast with goofy grins on our faces. Fortunately for both of us, no one paid us any mind. I was thrilled when just about the entire group decided to go on an outing. They had been discussing the old plantation ruins and everyone wanted to go but Annie and Liz, who seemed to be at odds that morning. They decided to spend their day at the beach.

Once the van made its way down the drive, Adrienne and I met with our fellow conspirators to determine what new task we would assign Hank to. Adrienne came up with the perfect idea: we would have Hank inspect the roof of each cottage and spray for pests. Shelby and I decided that we would be the ones to pay his shack a visit and do some snooping.

Neither Adrienne nor Myra were happy with the arrangements, but I explained that Adrienne was always more persuasive with Hank and would be more likely to get him to do what we wanted. The plan was to let him get started for a while and then Shelby and I would wander off. About an hour later, Hank stomped into the bar.

"Good morning, Hank," Adrienne said nonchalantly. "I'm terribly sorry to bother you this early in the day, but we had a snake get into one of the cottages last night. Would you please inspect the roofing on each of the cottages for snakes and spray them down for pests today? I don't want any of our guests having any more unwanted visitors showing up in the night."

Hank grunted in agreement and mumbled something under his breath about pesticide. He wandered off toward the laundry cottage and emerged shortly after with a canister and a ladder. Once he had mixed the chemicals and climbed up on the first cottage, Shelby and I set off for his place.

I silently prayed when we entered the old, dilapidated shack that Hank would not decide to take a break and return before he finished the spray job to find us rummaging through his belongings. It didn't come as a surprise to either me or Shelby that Hank was a complete pig. His place was strewn with beer cans and containers of rotting food. We did our best not to disturb anything, but the place was such a trash heap that even if we did, he'd never notice. I was really feeling the fool and had almost given up the search after we'd found nothing but piles of dirty clothes. We were on our way out the door when I tripped over a satchel halfway buried under trash and his nasty laundry.

Shelby glanced at me and opened the latch. Our eyes widened at the neatly stacked piles of cash inside. Shelby's hands trembled as she pulled out a wad of bills. "Hayden, why would a man living like this have this much cash lying around?"

We replaced it exactly how we had found it and made a hasty retreat. After taking the long way around to the inn, we were breathless when we arrived at the bar. It was a few minutes before we could tell Adrienne and Myra what we had found.

"It's money he's looking for!" I said breathlessly. "Apparently, he has money buried on the premises. We found a bag covered in dirt and sand and it was filled with cash. He's got to have more bags buried around here, that's why he's still digging, and the big dumb-ass pirate either didn't make a map or he lost it and he can't figure out where he buried the treasure—"

"Hayden, slow down, honey. Here, drink this." She handed Shelby and me a couple of bottles of cold water. "Now, we know that if and when he finds that money, he'll vanish. We have to get busy on our digging."

When Shelby and I had gotten our strength back, we decided to install one of the new flowerbeds. The only problem was that Hank had a bird's eye view of our work. If we did find anything, we would have to do something with it discreetly.

We all met in the courtyard to go over the sketches that I'd made. I'd gone to great lengths to come up with something that would blend in with the other landscaping and not stand out like a sore thumb.

Bless Calvin; he had delivered a dozen fifty-pound bags of potting soil the day before, although he did charge me out the ass for them. I took a spray can and marked off the design of the new bed, and we had just broken the surface of the ground when Hank approached and inquired as to what we were doing.

My heart skipped a beat when I heard his voice, but I did my best to sound casual. "Oh, you know, Hank, I've got landscaping in my blood. I couldn't help but throw in a new bed or two here and there. How are things going with the roofing?"

"Got two more cottages to go, and I'll be done. Do you ladies need help with your project?"

"Oh no, Hank." I waved my hand and my glove flew off and hit him in the chest. "You've done more than you know by assuring me that there were no snakes up there. We girls are just doing this to keep ourselves in shape, but thank you just the same for the kind offer."

He grunted in his usual fashion and handed me my glove. "If you need anything, just holler," he said before walking off.

We breathed a collective sigh of relief when he was far enough away. "Do you think he is on to us?" Myra asked as she scraped away the sprouts of grass within our work area.

"I think he's a little suspicious. We rarely ever do things like this when we have guests," Adrienne said.

Once we had cleared the area of brush and grass, we plunged our shovels deep into the sandy soil. We broke up every inch of dirt within the perimeter I had marked off but found nothing. The new bed turned out beautifully, so even though we'd turned up zip, at least all of our hard work produced something positive.

That night after dinner we sat around the bar, drained from the hard labor and being in the sun all day. Thank God our guests were equally tired from their adventure, and we all went to our cottages a little after midnight.

"He was stoned when he buried the money," Adrienne said suddenly as we lay in bed. "I can hear him cursing himself for it in my mind. Hayden, there's a lot of money buried out there." She turned to look me in the eye.

"This is like searching for a needle in a haystack. We don't have any better chance of finding it than he does at this rate." The frustration was wearing me thin.

Adrienne looked as though she was about to speak when she stared off again. "He's bothered by our sudden interest in gardening. He plans to get a metal detector."

I was amazed at her ability to eavesdrop into Hank's ponderings. Once he got that detector, there would be no stopping him. However, he would have to be very creative in finding a way to use it without being noticed.

"Shit! I wish there was some way we could get Colie to have him under surveillance when he goes on the hunt. Right now I'm certain he thinks I'm some paranoid nutcase." I got up and began to pace.

Adrienne watched me for a moment. "We have to catch him in the act, and then we can get Colie to do something about it. Myra and Shelby have a video camera. We can take turns keeping an eye on him. Now come to bed, I'm in a cuddling mood." She lifted the covers, inviting me in, and I wasted no time jumping into bed and her arms.

The next day began like any other. We all met for breakfast in the dining room. Billy was in an especially antagonistic mood and decided to rail on me. Of course, in the interest of being a good hostess, I gave as good as I got.

He drank his coffee, looking directly at me the whole time as if daring me to say something. "I don't know if I can recommend this place to anyone back home. After all, you've had a guest turn up missing, the plumbing has backed up, and a snake found its way into one of the cottages. Tell me, Hayden, is it always this exciting here?" He chuckled nervously after he finished speaking.

I pushed my plate away and leaned back in my chair, taking a calming breath before responding to his snide question. The entire room fell silent, and everyone watched us as though they were at a tennis match. "I have to agree with you, Billy. It seems we have had quite a few problems this go-around. I guess you're like a bad luck charm."

"I think you ladies need a man around here to run things, someone who can take care of the maintenance of the place." Again he let loose a chuckle and refused to look me in the eye as he spoke.

"I would think you, being a gay man, would realize that we no more need a man to take care of us than you and Chris need a woman around your home. At least, I assume the two of you get along just fine without female assistance. I do have to say, I figure you to be the type to still be living at home with his mommy." I grinned at that one.

He set his cup down and chuckled again. The chuckle was really getting on my nerves. Was he unable to have a conversation without that idiotic little laugh? He never looked me in the eyes either, which told me that he was insecure and made me despise him all the more.

"It's a proven fact that men can survive without a woman around, but women can't always do what men can do."

"Such as?"

"Repairs, heavy lifting, and of course peeing while standing." This time Richard chuckled.

"Most of the repairs around here are done by Adrienne, Iris, and me. Anything we choose not to do, we delegate to

Hank. As far as heavy lifting, there is always a way to work around that when you use your head. I always pee standing up in public restrooms, so you'll have to come up with something better than that."

I cut him off before he could speak. "Don't misunderstand me, Billy. I do not dislike men in general. I respect a man who can look me in the eye and say what's on his mind, but I have no use for weak men—or women, for that matter."

"Hayden, I can show you a real man if you want." The nervous chuckle was a little louder on that one.

"Well, Billy, when you go into town to pick up a real man, let me know. I need a few things from the market." A broad grin broke across my face, and I continued to stare at him waiting for him to meet my eyes. The room was silent except for Billy's nervous chuckle. The women of the group all stared at Billy in contempt, waiting for him to say something else. Chris finally came to his lover's rescue.

"Hayden, tell me, is it true there's a pretty decent reef that we can access from the beach here? We were thinking about doing some snorkeling later."

Adrienne nodded. "There's a beautiful reef right off the beach here. We have plenty of snorkel equipment for anyone who would like to have a look. Hayden and I have snorkeled it many times and would be happy to show you around."

I was not happy about being volunteered to snorkel with Billy. I figured the chubby bastard would pee in the water any time he was near me. I was not going to let Adrienne suffer alone, though, so I went with the group.

As I had suspected, Billy was lazy and lay on the beach while the rest of us explored the reef. It was his loss. Some of the most beautiful scenery in the Caribbean was found beneath its crystal-clear waters. I never tired of admiring the beauty of the corals and sea life.

I was standing on a sandbar adjusting my mask when Chris swam over and joined me. "Hayden, I really am sorry about Billy's remarks earlier. He gets in these moods, and he tries to find someone to bully. Personally, I think the inn is beautiful, and you ladies do a fine job of managing it. Maybe some day I'll come back without Billy."

"That's really sweet of you to say. I hope you'll forgive my bluntness, but I'm amazed at how different you and Billy are. I guess it's true about opposites attracting."

"He's a different person altogether when we're alone." Chris ran his fingers through his thinning hair. "I'll be honest, though, those times are getting few and far between. I don't want to break his heart, but I'm having a problem coping with his bravado in public. He's really not the jerk he pretends so hard to be."

Chris and I stuck close together as we explored the reef. I really enjoyed his company, and with his obnoxious mate sleeping on the beach we all got to see the vibrant personality that Chris kept hidden in Billy's presence. It saddened me to know that such a sweet person was overshadowed by someone hell-bent on being an ass.

During the hottest part of the day, the group dispersed to nap or lounge on the beach. Adrienne showered and then fell asleep across our bed. Normally, I would be first in line for a nap, but I just couldn't make myself lie down. I paced around the cottage for a little while and then decided to pay my beloved aunt a visit.

I grabbed a small basket and filled it with fresh flowers I picked as I walked along the road to the cemetery. Aunt Gloria's grave and tombstone were already covered in flowers. I cleared away some of the wilted ones and replaced them with the fresh flowers that I had picked. I had never seen a grave site so adorned. My aunt was greatly loved. I sat down in the soft grass next to her grave and breathed in the sweet fragrance of the fresh new flowers as I spoke to her.

"Good afternoon, Auntie G. It sure would be nice if you were still here with us. I could use your wisdom in this situation with Hank. I'm to the point of wishing he would just find the money and hightail it out of here. I know that's not fair to Brandon, but I'm worried about the safety of those I've come to love. You always said everything happens for a reason; I hope one day I'll understand why all of this has happened."

I took another deep breath and raised my face up to the bright sunlight. "I wanted to thank you for all you left for me. The inn is great, but I think you know I'm really talking about Adrienne. Some mornings when I wake up before she does, I just roll over and look at her face, sometimes for almost an hour, just looking at her. She is so beautiful. There's nothing more intriguing to me than a woman who likes being a woman and isn't ashamed of all of her feminine qualities. Of course, I'm sure you know that."

I laughed out loud, thinking how silly I must look sitting there talking to the dirt and flowers, but I didn't care. My aunt was buried there, and it made me feel close to her. Even though I knew that my aunt's spirit had been set free of its earthly bonds, I could feel her presence. "Anyway, I just wanted to thank you for bringing such a beautiful person into my life. She says she loves me, ya know." I grinned, then got up and headed back to the inn—my home.

"Where have you been, my love? I was beginning to get worried about you," Adrienne said when I joined her in the bar.

I took her in my arms and hugged her, then kissed her without worrying who might be watching. She smiled at me with a questioning look in her eyes.

"I went to visit Gloria's grave. I needed to thank her for bringing someone so wonderful into my life." I kissed her again and made up my mind that later that night I would show her just how wonderful I thought she was.

Dinner was pleasant for a change, and Billy seemed to make an effort at behaving himself. It wasn't near as much fun as it had been with our previous guests, and I knew it never would be. Those girls were a different experience altogether.

After dinner, most of the guests returned to their cottages. Billy and Chris and the Burkes settled down to a game of poker. Myra and Shelby joined Adrienne and me for drinks, and Adrienne filled them in on Hank's intentions. Both quickly agreed to work with us by roaming the grounds at night keeping an eye out for Hank. Shelby agreed to let us use her video camera, and our plan was set.

While Adrienne talked to our friends, I ran my fingertips lazily up and down her thigh. I could tell the effect my actions were having by the tiny goose bumps rising up on her skin. Occasionally, she would cast me a sideways glance, but I continued undaunted. Matter of fact, the more she glanced my way, the higher I let my fingertips roam. The fact that she'd chosen to wear a skirt that night made my explorations all the more interesting.

She grabbed my hand before I could get to the spot where I truly wanted to be and gave me a grin. Billy, apparently, had a few bad hands of cards dealt to him and decided to throw in the towel. The Burkes followed, retiring for the night as well. With Shelby and Myra helping us straighten up the bar, we were all off toward our cottages in record time.

"What exactly were you trying to do to me back there, Hayden?" Adrienne asked, squeezing my hand as we walked to the cottage.

"Ah, my love, if you don't know then I have a lot to teach you, and we can start those lessons tonight." I pulled her into a little grove of trees and kissed her, teasingly nipping at her bottom lip. She intertwined her fingers in my hair in an attempt to kiss me deeper. I ran my fingers slowly up her thighs until her breath came in gasps.

"Not here, Hayden, let's go inside," Adrienne panted against my neck.

"No. Let's do it right here, right now." I ran my hands up under her skirt and stroked her through her panties. She groaned at my touch. "I don't think you really want me to stop now anyway," I whispered as I nibbled her ear.

She leaned against the tree and wrapped her arms around my neck as I kissed her. At first I tried to work around her underwear, but when it became frustrating I ripped the thin material off her. I moaned when I ran my fingers between her legs and realized how aroused she was.

I kissed her neck and slid my fingers into her. Her grip on my shoulders tightened. Running my tongue around her ear, I whispered, "Don't make a sound, not one sound, or I will tease you mercilessly."

The strokes were slow and deep, and I took great pleasure feeling her body shudder each time I filled her. I kissed her again, sucking her tongue into my mouth as I pulled out of her and began to stroke her clit. Her knees trembled, and she was forced to put more of her weight on me as she wrapped her arms tighter around my neck. With each stroke, I whispered in her ear all the things I planned to do to her that night. When her breath caught in her throat and her hips stilled, I smiled against her ear.

I led her on shaky legs toward our cottage. "I have so much more in mind for you tonight, my love," I said, then opened the door. After undressing her just inside of the doorway, I led her to the bed.

"Get on the bed and get down on your knees." She did as I asked without a word of protest. I knelt behind her and tangled my fingers into her hair, pushing her head down onto the pillow. I entered her slowly, grinning at the groan she released into the pillow.

I took her slowly at first, moving as her hips dictated, but when she whispered, "Please don't stop, Hayden," I lost all control and the desire to be gentle. My strokes became hard and fast. I watched as she clutched the pillow, and I listened to her scream into it. Without warning, she pulled her body straight up and leaned back into me, slinging her long hair over my shoulders and face.

She gasped twice, and her breathing stilled again as she laid her head back on my shoulder. "Don't move, Hayden," she whispered breathlessly. I stayed perfectly still, feeling her spasm against my fingers. When she was spent I laid her back onto the bed and held her until her breathing became normal again.

When she began to run her fingertips across my stomach, I grabbed her hand. "No, my love, my desires are satisfied for this evening. All I want you to do is drift off to sleep in my arms and tell everybody at breakfast tomorrow that I rolled your eyes up in your head again. Especially Billy."

"I never know what is going to come out of that mouth of yours, Hayden." She settled her head down on my shoulder, and we fell into a contented sleep. But in the morning, I would have to tell her she talked in her sleep. I had no idea what she had meant by "two down and three more to go."

CHAPTER TWELVE

Good morning, Monkey Chops," Shelby greeted us brightly as Adrienne and I strolled into the bar a good hour after breakfast.

"Billy and Chris went down to the beach. The others have all gone into town with one of the porters to go souvenir shopping. Looks like we have the place to ourselves for a while, which is good because you two don't look like you slept that much last night," Myra said with a wink.

I couldn't help but laugh. Adrienne's face turned a dark crimson, confirming what Myra and Shelby obviously suspected. We sat down and Adrienne quickly changed the subject, which we all found even more amusing.

Shelby sighed. "I'm afraid we fell asleep last night and didn't keep our vigil. We never discussed who would be taking the first patrol yesterday."

"Well, we kind of fell down on the job too; I had other things in mind when we turned in last night." Adrienne's face turned red again at my remark.

"Since you two were up late last night playing slap and tickle, why don't you take a nap today and take the first round tonight. Myra and I will take it up tomorrow night," Shelby suggested as she sipped her coffee.

"Sounds like a great plan to me." I smirked. "I got quite a workout last night and could use a little more sleep." That earned me a playful slap.

Adrienne and I ate a late breakfast, and then went back to bed. Unlike the night before, we actually did sleep. In fact, we managed to sleep nearly the whole day away and woke up only an hour before dinner. Refreshed from a shower and a whole day's sleep, we felt invigorated.

At dinner that night we listened to the group tell of their shopping adventure. Souvenir shops were sparse on the island, but everyone had managed to find what they were looking for. Abigail and Sandy bought some baskets from the local basket makers who even gave them an impromptu class on weaving. I didn't even entertain the group by exchanging barbs with Billy—it didn't seem worth the effort since I'd be rid of the bespectacled pestilence in only a few days anyway. The chatter around the table was lighthearted. Until Billy brought up Brandon Fallon.

"You still haven't told us about that Brandon guy that disappeared the first night here," he said around a mouthful of food.

I was beginning to wonder about dear ol' Billy. He didn't behave like a gay man, but I have never been one to stereotype. Something about him got on my last nerve, and his curiosity about Brandon made me seriously wonder if Hank had an accomplice.

Not wanting a replay of early conversations, Adrienne jumped in before I could answer. "The authorities have been notified. We've been very concerned for Mr. Fallon, but aside from reporting him missing, there is very little we can do."

"Have you tried contacting his family to see if they've heard from him?" Billy was obviously going to press the issue.

"No, we haven't, but we did give his emergency contact information to the Bahamian police," Adrienne answered, a lot more politely than I would have.

"I guess that's all you can do, then," Billy said.

Chris jumped in. "Hayden, every now and then when you speak I detect a slight accent. Is it Cajun?"

"I was born and raised in Louisiana, but my family is not of Cajun French descent. If you live with real Cajuns long enough, it's hard to keep that accent out of your speech."

"Adrienne, are you from Louisiana also?" Jerri asked as she gave my love a smile that was all too reminiscent of Dana's. I was not going through that mess again. If this woman decided to get a little too frisky I was gonna bitch slap her, guest or not!

"I'm from Florida, Miami to be exact," Adrienne answered politely.

"Miami? They have a lot of problems with drugs down there, don't they?" Billy piped up again.

"No more than anywhere else, I would suppose. Then again, I wouldn't know much about it since I came here relatively young. My wild, youthful years were spent here on the island."

I wondered where Billy was going with his line of questioning, but he let it drop before it could go further. I glanced over at Myra and Shelby, whose perplexed expressions mirrored my own. Billy's behavior was becoming stranger by the minute.

After dinner, Adrienne and I excused ourselves to walk the grounds. We strolled hand in hand, trying our best to look casual while keeping an eye out for Hank. When we passed the small grove of trees that we'd spent time in the previous night, I watched as a smile graced Adrienne's face.

"What is going through that beautiful head of yours, my love?" I asked, squeezing her hand.

"Oh, just fond memories, that's all."

I stopped in my tracks and spun her around. "Would you like a replay of last night?" I said in between kisses.

"As much as I love the sound of that, I can't watch for Hank with my eyes rolled up in my head." She giggled.

"Why would you be watching for me?" A male voice came from the shadows.

All the blood drained from my body as I stood there holding Adrienne's hands in mine. Her eyes grew wide with the realization that Hank was standing only a few feet from us. I swallowed hard when I saw Hank emerge from the shadows.

I stammered as I tried to think of a way to lie my way out of the situation. "Hank! We, um, were talking about something else."

"Cut the shit, Hayden, I heard you both. Now before either of you get the bright idea to scream, you better realize I don't have a thing to lose by killing you both. I'm a dead man anyway."

I felt nauseous when I saw the moonlight reflect off the blade of the knife he held. Adrienne's eyes easily conveyed what she was thinking. I shook my head, telling her it was not a good idea to try and run.

He stepped up beside Adrienne and took her by the arm. "Let's take a walk back to my place, ladies."

My mind raced with ideas of escape as we walked to his shack, but he was too close to Adrienne and the fear of her getting hurt terrified me. He shoved us through the door of his house and made us sit down on his disgusting bed while he sat in a chair in front of us.

"I knew I shoulda took that first bag of money and run, got my sorry ass back to Galveston, but of course I had to go and get greedy. There are three more bags out there that I ain't even got to yet. I coulda sneaked back onta the island and got 'em later, but no. With you two silly bitches nosin' around in the dark like a pig rootin' out a grub worm and then digging up the whole damn place like confounded armadillos, I was forced to change my mind."

"Hank, just take what you have and go. We won't say a word to anyone—" Adrienne stammered before Hank cut her off.

"Give me a break, Adrienne! We all know better than that! That Harry Potter–looking bastard you have staying with you has been asking about me all over town. I shoulda took care of him just like I did ol' Brandon. I knew they'd send more than one guy to look for me. That money is mine! They screwed me over so many times I oughta be walking bowlegged. And I sure as hell didn't enjoy a minute of it, so I just took what them bastards owed me. All this time I been out here in the middle of bumfuck, ain't a one of 'em found me 'til now.

"That fat bastard'll kill ever one'a you at this inn to get his hands on that money. Didn't neither of you two realize it, but your days were numbered when him and that Fallon set foot on Cat Island. Whether I kill ya or he does, the difference ain't worth a tinker's damn 'cause you both gonna die. 'Cepting with me, it'll be quick."

Adrienne and I sat dumbfounded. We watched in stunned silence as he opened up a briefcase and took out several passports. As he opened each one, I was amazed to see a clean-cut Hank, minus the eye patch, in each picture.

"Clever disguise."

"Oh, this ain't no disguise. I lost my eye when I staged the boat accident the day I took the money." He flipped up the patch to reveal an empty eye socket. Adrienne and I recoiled at the grisly sight.

"Smug bastards! I knew they'd figure out I staged it when they couldn't find hide nor hair of the money. I'd planned on being a damn sight farther away from here by this time, but my injuries kept me from making it off the island. I paid off the local medicine man to keep him shut up and happy, but I reckon they musta either paid him more or beat it out of him.

"When I was well enough, I buried the money around the inn. I stayed so kidney-rippin' stoned for the first few months because of the pain that I can't remember where I hid the rest of the money. There's still a half million dollars buried out there, and I won't ever be able to find it, but I'll be damned if I let them sonsabitches find me."

He got up and began to pace back and forth through the mess that was his cottage. I looked around the room for something to use as a weapon and came up with nothing but empty beer cans. I was afraid that Myra and Shelby would come looking for us but was more frightened by the thought of them being in the presence of a killer as ruthless as Hank.

"Now you two listen up and do what I say, and I promise that when you die, I'll make it quick and painless. We're gonna to take a little ride down to the marina." He handed us each a satchel while he carried the knife and the briefcase. Adrienne and I did as we were ordered and carried the cases to the Jeep. As I lifted mine to put it in the old vehicle, I used all of my weight and slammed it into Hank's face.

"Run, Adrienne!" I screamed, and we both bolted off into the darkness. Adrienne blazed a trail through the brush with me quick on her heels. The blow to Hank was enough to knock him off his feet, but he was quickly closing in on us. I could hear his heavy footsteps coming up behind me and I veered off the trail.

He did as I had hoped, thinking he could catch the slower of us. It was a good choice on his part because all those years of smoking came to roost. My chest heaved and burned, and exhaustion threatened to overtake the adrenaline that came with sheer terror. I could see the lights of the inn through the trees and mustered all the energy I had to make it there, but when I could hear Hank panting just behind me I dropped to the ground in a ball, causing him to trip over me and fall headlong into the brush.

I got up again and tried to run. My back ached where Hank's knees had connected with it, and I wheezed as I tried to fill my lungs with air. Hank caught me by the hair and slung me to the ground, and before I could struggle free from his grasp he pressed the knife blade to my throat.

"You stupid bitch!" he spat. "You're gonna be responsible for everybody in that inn dying tonight!"

My heart sank with the fear of what Adrienne had run into back at the inn. I closed my eyes and prayed that Billy and Chris had already gone to bed for the night. Hank pulled me to my feet by my hair and pressed the knife so close to my throat I thought he had already cut me.

"Let her go, Hank!" Adrienne stood panting before us with a branch in her hand, poised to strike.

"Don't do anything dumber than you already have, Adrienne. I'll slit her throat and cut yours before she ever hits the ground. Drop that stick and come with me, and I mean now!"

Even in the darkness, I could see Adrienne weighing her options. I know it was selfish, but I wanted him to kill me first. I didn't want to see him harm her.

"Run, Adrienne! Run and warn the others!" I cried as he pressed the knife harder against my throat.

"Don't be stupid, Adrienne! You know I'll kill her if you do. Do you wanna witness what that assassin'll do to your precious Iris and the rest of your friends?" Hank pressed the knife harder against my throat, and I could feel the blade cutting into my skin, releasing a small trickle of blood to run down my neck.

I closed my tearing eyes and yelled. "Run, Adrienne!"

A strange noise rang out into the night, and I felt my body sink down as Hank's unconscious form collapsed to the ground. Adrienne grabbed me and pulled me into her arms, and I kept my eyes clamped closed, afraid to open them. Then I heard the strange noise again, and three more times after that.

"Oh God, Iris," Adrienne moaned.

I opened my eyes to see Iris standing over a very dead Hank. Blood dripped from the cast iron skillet she often used to cook in, and we were all three covered in crimson splatter marks. I was reminded that no matter how much we were already paying Iris, it wasn't nearly enough.

"Drop the skillet, lady!" a male voice shouted. I looked up to see Chris aiming a pistol at Iris. "Drop it now!"

Suddenly all the things Hank had said about Billy rang through my head. We were still in deep shit. Faster than I ever thought I could manage, I grabbed the branch that Adrienne had been holding and hit Chris behind the knees, sending him to the ground with a thud. Adrienne was on him in a heartbeat, trying to wrestle the gun from his grip.

Instinctively, I knew that the footsteps I heard running toward me belonged to Billy. With all that I had left in me, I swung around with the branch and caught him across the jaw. His feet flew out from under him, and he hit the ground in a gelatinous heap.

Iris had joined Adrienne in the fight for Chris's gun and was working his lower body over good with the skillet. We looked like a modern-day version of the Keystone Kops. I stumbled over to Chris and stomped his wrist, grinding it into the ground, until he finally released the gun.

"I will splatter your brains out all over this ground if you move another muscle!" I shouted as I aimed the gun at his face. He froze and stared back up at me, confused.

"Adrienne, find Billy's gun, and Iris, go call Colie," I ordered as I stared into Chris's eyes with murderous intent in my heart. Adrienne found Billy's gun and stood guard over him.

Chris tried to reason with me. "Hayden, we are DEA. We were sent here to follow Brandon Fallon."

"You're lying!" I spat at him. "You were working with Fallon, and I'm not going to let you harm anyone here. Matter of fact, I may start shooting your toes off one by one because of what you are."

"Hayden, I swear, we're DEA. Look inside my wallet and you'll find my credentials." He slowly moved his hand closer to his body.

"Did you get confused when I told you not to move a muscle? I wasn't joking when I said I would blow your brains out!" My nerves were beginning to fray, and I actually toyed with the idea of shooting him in the leg to just show him I wasn't farting around.

"Hayden." Adrienne's voice was smooth and calming. "I think he's telling the truth. Look at this." She handed me Billy's wallet, and there inside was his ID.

"What if this is fake and we surrender to them? I'm not moving a muscle until Colie gets here, and then he can take over." I glared back at Chris. "That is, if they don't do something stupid and I have to unload this gun into them both."

Iris came running across the yard, yelling at the top of her lungs. "Colie's on the way, and he says not to hurt the policemen!"

I still glared down at Chris. I had come too close to getting killed, and I was reluctant to relinquish the gun. Shelby and Myra came running behind Iris and stared wide-eyed at the three men sprawled out on the ground before us. Their expressions grew even wider when they noticed the guns we had trained down on them.

Shelby approached me slowly, focusing on my blood-smeared neck. "Hayden, you're hurt. I need to take a look at that cut."

"Nobody is looking at a damn thing 'til Colie gets here!" I managed to yell. "Only when he gets here will I put this gun down! Now everybody stay back."

The doctor in Shelby rose to the surface. "Can I at least take a look at Hank and Billy?" she asked timidly.

"Yes," I answered, as calmly as I could muster.

She knelt down over Billy and felt for a pulse. He was out cold but alive. She moved over to Hank but didn't even bother to check him; the mortal injuries were obvious. "What the hell happened to him?" she asked as she stood.

"Ol' Faithful happened to dat ol' boy," Iris grinned proudly. "Gloria told me, 'Always take care of my girls, Iris,' and I made that promise. When Adrienne found me tonight the first thing I grabbed was my skillet, and I kept my promise."

Colie arrived shortly after with several men who identified themselves as DEA agents. I handed the gun over and allowed one of them to lead us back to the bar where Shelby tended to the bleeding cut on my throat. Adrienne sat beside me, holding my hand as we answered all of the questions the agent asked us.

We allowed the agents to use our bar as a makeshift command center for their investigation. We were questioned over and over until the sun began to rise. The other guests had already filed into the bar to see what the commotion was about and were questioned as well.

After the interrogation, we were all allowed to return to our cottages and get some rest. When I went into the bathroom, I was shocked at the reflection staring back at me. I was wild eyed with exhaustion. My hair was filled with sand and twigs. There was a nasty-looking gash across my throat that I was surprised did not need stitches. I looked and felt like hammered shit.

Adrienne had already turned the shower on, and we showered together, not wanting to be separated for even a minute. I didn't remember falling asleep, only being led to the bed. When we finally woke up, it was well after lunch.

"Hayden, did I dream what happened last night?" Adrienne asked groggily. She propped herself up on one elbow and looked at my neck. "No, it was real," she said as she stared at the cut across my throat.

"Nope, it wasn't a dream, but now it's all over, and we don't have to worry about Hank anymore." I ran my fingers through her hair. Silently, I thanked God that I still had Adrienne alive and well.

We got up and showered and went straight to the bar. Iris had taken a short nap, then got up early and had been cooking for Colie and the DEA agents all day. Our staff, assisted by Myra and Shelby, had tended to all our guests in our absence. A lump rose up in my throat as I considered the people I was surrounded by.

Sitting at one of the tables were Billy and Chris, Billy sporting a bruise that dominated the right side of his face. He glared at Adrienne and me as we walked into the bar. Snickers could be heard amongst the group of agents.

"So...is it safe to assume you two are not lovers?" I said as I approached their table. Billy continued to glare at me, and Chris spoke up.

"No, Miss Tate, I thought I made that clear last night," Chris responded in a very snide tone, which immediately pissed me off. Had they made their presence known we would have never endangered ourselves or stuck our noses in their business.

"Well, Chrissy boy, had you made that clear before last night, you might not have gotten an ass whipping with a skillet," I retorted. The agents surrounding us laughed openly.

"We were conducting an official investigation that you should not have involved yourselves in," Chris said through clenched teeth.

"We would have never gotten involved had we known about you two. Although we wouldn't have put a lot of faith in you since you lost the man you were investigating the first night you arrived!"

Adrienne gently tugged my arm, trying to calm me down, and some of the other agents stepped between Chris and me and made me go to my corner. I was seething with anger at the position they had put us in.

"Come sit down, Slugger," Shelby said as she pulled my chair out. She put a plate of food in front of me, but I was so angry I couldn't eat. Adrienne did, though; she went at her plate like a woman who hadn't eaten in a year.

Shelby put an arm over my shoulders and gave me a smile. "Calm down, my friend. I think you two punished those bums enough. Have you noticed that Billy is being uncharacteristically quiet?"

"Now that you mention it, he didn't throw in his two cents the whole time," I said, glancing over my shoulder at him.

"I think you may have broken his jaw. He won't let me look at it and barely speaks at all. He hasn't had a bite to eat all day."

I began to feel bad for Billy. True, he was a grade-A, certified ass and had decided to make a vacation out of his investigation, which nearly got us killed. Still, I felt a little sorry for him. It must have been very emasculating for him to be bested by a trio of women armed with a skillet and a stick.

I also noticed that Chris walked with a limp. Iris must have really done a number on his knee. I could see the bruising on his wrist from where I had stomped on it. I would have hated being in either of their shoes; they both would probably be riding desks real soon.

The one bright spot in all of this mess was that Iris and Colie seemed to really hit it off. He followed her around like a lost puppy, and she doted on him every chance she got. We got a kick out of watching them exchange glances and smiles when they thought no one was looking. They reminded me of two teenagers.

There was even more questioning and statements to be signed. It seemed that when Brandon Fallon was dispatched to the island, the DEA already were moving in on the men who controlled his organization. They had been arrested the previous morning for a list of charges, not the least of which was murder.

We still had to prepare for the early departure of our guests, minus two whom I personally would have loved to send packing. The evening was a flurry of activity. When we were finally able to sit down and take a break, it was two a.m. Shelby and Myra joined Adrienne and me in doing some serious damage to a bottle of spiced rum.

"I still can't get over the fact that I didn't know Billy and Chris were DEA," Adrienne confessed as she rubbed her glass against her forehead. "Well, I never professed to be totally accurate."

"They weren't very good agents, if that helps any," Myra said.

"They weren't even really good at being gay, either," Shelby added with a laugh.

"I propose a toast," I said as I raised my glass. "To Iris, who wields a mean skillet. May we never incur her wrath."

The following evening after all of the guests were gone, we threw a party for the staff, and even invited Colie. Iris was the guest of honor and allowed me to have dominion over the barbecue. We ate and danced and partied like there was no tomorrow. A weight had been lifted off our shoulders, and a feeling of peace and contentment settled back over the inn.

The DEA agents finally left us, taking with them the bruised and battered Billy and Chris. I did bring myself to utter a half-assed apology for the thrashing we gave them. Neither of them seemed impressed. Billy simply grunted his good-bye, which was the nicest conversation I'd ever had with him.

My heart was broken the day Shelby and Myra left for home. They assured us they'd be back soon and promised to keep us updated on their progress.

One morning as Adrienne and I sat leisurely in the bar sipping our coffee, Adrienne looked up at me with an odd expression. "Hayden, go get the cordless phone. Your mom is about to call."

I did as she suggested. When I sat back down at the table the phone rang in my hand. "Hi, Mom," I answered, and listened as she began to instantly rattle off complaints about me not calling her.

"Hayden, your dad and I have been talking, and we want you to come home for Christmas. Your brother and his wife have already agreed to come, and we want you here too. Are you taking care of yourself, hon? I'm sure you're regular since they mostly have only fruit over there, but are you getting any protein? Have you been taking care of your teeth?"

I set the phone down and lit a cigarette. I could hear her voice steadily coming out of the phone like a buzzing bee. I sighed and took a sip of my coffee before putting the phone back up to my ear. Adrienne watched in amusement.

"Mom...I...listen...Mom...sheesh." I put the phone down again and continued to smoke and sip my coffee. The buzzing continued to pour out of the phone and when it stopped for a breath, I picked the phone up quickly. "Mom, I'll think about Christmas, okay? Love-ya-bye-bye."

When I set the phone down, I looked into a pair of beautiful green eyes.

"Yes."

"Yes what?" I asked in confusion.

"Yes, I will go home with you for Christmas, but I can tell you right now that I don't like your brother," Adrienne said with a smile.

I patted her hand. "That's okay, my love. I don't like him much myself, and don't get me started on that wife of his. Her name is Wanda, and she has these big oogly eyes and—are you sure you want to put yourself through that?" I asked when her eyes rolled up into her head.

"I have to go with you to make sure you come back to the island," she batted back playfully.

"You don't have to worry about that, my love. You're stuck with me for life." I kissed her.

We were happy about the early departure of the guests and used the time to recuperate emotionally and physically. We cleaned out Hank's old shack and threw away nearly everything in it, giving away the rest to anybody that would have it. As for the shack, I burned that bitch to the ground.

Iris and Colie became a hot item. The four of us spent many an evening at the inn dining together on the open patio. I saw a vibrant side to Iris I didn't even know existed. When Adrienne and I forced her out, Colie would take her out on his boat or shopping in Nassau. Our extended family had gained another member, and we welcomed him with open arms.

I was glad that Iris was going to have someone with her when Adrienne and I went to the States in a few months for Christmas. I planned on bringing back many gifts for my new family. But I already had the best gift I would ever get, and she would be going home with me to meet the parents.

There is one part I forgot to mention. The entire time we were being interrogated, we never mentioned the half million dollars to Colie and the boys. The only money they found was what Hank had uncovered and was trying to take with him.

The rest of it—well, let's just say that Cat Island has a mighty fine medical facility in the planning stages right now. It's about time that drug money got cycled back to the community. Aunt Gloria always said that things happen for a reason. She was right. The people of Cat Island would reap the benefits of Hank's actions for a long time to come.

Adrienne and I now have grandkittens. Saber found himself a beautiful mate, a cream-colored long-haired kind of girl. He and his beloved sleep at our feet each night, along with all six of their children. They don't call this place Cat Island for nothing.

About the Author

Born in 1965, Robin Alexander grew up in Baton Rouge, Louisiana, where she still resides. An avid reader of lesbian fiction, Robin decided to take the leap and try her hand at writing, which is now her favorite hobby. Other favorites are camping, snorkeling, and anything to do with the outdoors or the water. Robin approaches everything with a sense of humor, which is evident in her style of writing.